Marriage Contract

On this day, Carlee Miller has agreed to marry millionaire Hal Ward, the father of her unborn child, despite the risk of falling in love with her handsome but temporary husband.

As the sole heir to the Ward fortune, the child will have every advantage in life.

The child's mother will want for nothing, either. (Though she may develop a longing for happily-ever-after with Hal....)

Bride *Carlee Miller*   Groom *Hal Ward*

Dear Reader,

This month we've got two wonderful books about pregnant heroines. I've never been pregnant myself, but these writers made it easy for me to see myself in their heroines' places. And what crazy circumstances each one of them finds herself facing.

Alexandra Sellers' *Shotgun Wedding* introduces us to Carlee Miller, happily planning a life with her about-to-be child—until she discovers there was a mix-up at the sperm bank. And now millionaire dad-to-be Hal Ward wants in on the action. And not just the diaper-changing action, either. Once this guy sets eyes on the mother of his child, he's looking forward to making his next baby the old-fashioned way.

For Libby Sinclair, heroine of Sandra Paul's *Baby on the Way,* it was the old-fashioned way that got her into trouble in the first place. And now Del Delaney, the other half of that troublemaking night, is back in town—just in time to crash Libby's baby shower and let her know there will be *lots* of nights just like it in her future. And for some reason, Libby's not complaining!

Enjoy them both, then come back next month for two more Yours Truly novels, the books all about unexpectedly meeting, dating—and marrying!—Mr. Right.

Yours,

Leslie Wainger

Leslie J. Wainger
Senior Editor and Editorial Coordinator

Please address questions and book requests to:
Silhouette Reader Service
U.S.: 3010 Walden Ave., P.O. Box 1325, Buffalo, NY 14269
Canadian: P.O. Box 609, Fort Erie, Ont. L2A 5X3

ALEXANDRA SELLERS

Shotgun Wedding

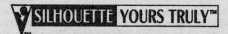

Published by Silhouette Books

America's Publisher of Contemporary Romance

This one's for you, Lynda

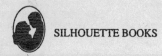

SILHOUETTE BOOKS

ISBN 0-373-52055-7

SHOTGUN WEDDING

Printed in U.S.A.

About the Author

The question people most often ask writers is, Where do you get your ideas? It's not always easy to answer, but Alexandra Sellers is in no doubt about where she first got the idea for *Shotgun Wedding*— from editor Lynda Curnyn. "Maybe you should write a sperm-bank story, Alexandra," Lynda said one day. "What's a sperm-bank story?" Alexandra asked, and by the time Lynda had explained, she was sold.

By chance, her legal eagle sister was on a visit, so it was only natural that the sperm-bank mix-ups recently in the news should get into the story. In fact, the first draft of the Cyberfuture letter was written by her sister, under instructions to be pompously legal. And as for Hal's occupation, Alexandra's husband is a car lover and an inventor in his spare time. Look for more of his inventions in a future Yours Truly novel, *Occupation Millionaire*.

Mix ingredients with a little imagination and a domineering old man, and that's how ideas happen. "Ideas are like wealth," according to Alexandra. "Some people get ideas, and some don't. But the world itself is absolutely rich with them."

Alexandra enjoys getting letters from readers, who can write her at P.O. Box 9449, London NW3 2WH, England.

Books by Alexandra Sellers

Silhouette Yours Truly

A Nice Girl Like You
Not Without a Wife!
Shotgun Wedding

Silhouette Intimate Moments

Prologue

The woman sat nervously holding her shoulder bag in her lap, her feet neatly together on the floor, and stared at the large pink and purple watercolor on the wall. She looked uncomfortable, but anyone would be, he reflected, submerged in this suffocatingly user-friendly decor. He was uncomfortable himself.

He'd been waiting twenty minutes, and she'd been here before him, so the outfit wasn't up to his grandfather's usual standards of efficiency. With any luck, he told himself with a wry grin, they'd screw up. He eased himself gently in the chair and cursed softly under his breath as pain from his ribs stabbed him. Damn the old man and his obsessions!

"Are you okay?" he heard, and looked up to see big blue eyes watching him with soft concern. She had heard him grunt.

He grinned reassurance at her. "I'll be fine."

"I guess you were in an accident," she said, flicking a glance from his bruised face to the cast on his arm.

Before he could answer, the receptionist came bustling self-importantly back into the room and sat down under the discreet sign that read, in white letters against a turquoise background, Cyberfuture. Planting seeds for the future. Underneath was another sign ordering them to please check in with the receptionist on arrival.

"I'm real sorry to keep you waiting, Mrs. Miller," she said. "Someone will be out for you soon."

"That's all right," said the woman, but as the man watched, she bit her lip, and he knew that the delay was affecting her. She looked like a kitten exploring outside the basket for the first time and nervous as hell about it.

He wondered where her husband was. If she was here for artificial insemination, he could imagine the husband having ego problems, but that was no excuse for leaving a woman like her to do it on her own. You could see by looking she was the kind of woman who needed protecting.

"Not very efficient," he observed, for the sake of getting another look at those blue eyes. She turned her head, but there was something behind her eyes when she looked at him that made him wonder what she disapproved of in him.

"I just hope my temperature stays up," she confided. He could see that she wasn't like any woman he'd ever met; or at least, none that he dated. A softly-rounded face to match the softly rounded body that made no attempt to disguise its femaleness; open, blue eyes; ruffled blond hair—which his expert eye told him had never fallen under the hand of a stylist of the calibre of Cantabria's celebrated Mr. Robert—and which she wore now in a ponytail that fell well down her back.

She had the fresh-faced, clean-living, open look of

someone always ready to pick up whatever hand life dealt her next, and he realized he was used to women who went after what they wanted. There was a shadow behind the blue eyes that said she had been hurt and had let the pain touch her. Himself, he preferred the self-assured gaze of sophisticated women who had learned to protect themselves.

She was attractive, all right, with a lot of sex appeal, but not his type at all. She needed looking after, and he wasn't the protective type.

"Mrs. Miller? Will you come this way, please?" said a girl who looked no more than eighteen, but who was wearing a nurse's uniform, and the woman smiled a friendly farewell at him and got up and followed the girl out.

Not a moment too soon, the man told himself in dry appreciation of his own weakness. Another minute and he'd have been offering her saddle room on his white horse.

1

20 June 1997

Mr. Harlan de Vouvray Ward IV
De Vouvray House
Cantabria, California

Dear Mr. de Vouvray Ward,
It is with much regret that we have to advise you that, due to unforeseen circumstances, the sperm that you placed on deposit with Cyberfuture on 15 May this year was inadvertently used in an insemination procedure that same day without your authorization.

The recipient is a client whose deceased husband's sperm was on deposit with us. There was an unfortunate confusion, and your own sperm was mistakenly used in the procedure in place of the correct specimen.

We hasten to assure you that your privacy has in no way been breached. We have taken and shall continue to take the utmost care to ensure that there will be no liability to you in the event that a pregnancy has resulted from the insemination procedure. We will not release to the recipient any personal details relating to you, although you will of course appreciate that in such an event pertinent medical information must be made available on health grounds. We have reason to believe that in this instance the Rh factor may be relevant.

We deeply regret this highly regrettable situation and trust that you will in no way be discomposed by it. Please be assured that Cyberfuture will continue to provide you with the best in service, efficiency and professionalism for the future.

Thank you for your understanding and cooperation in this matter.

Yours truly
G. Edgar Bloomer, Director
Cyberfuture Laboratories
Planting seeds for the future.

P.S. It will be necessary for you to drop into our clinic at your convenience and make a fresh deposit.

Hal Ward laughed. He was sitting in full sunshine, and the light haloing off the lightly curling gold-tipped hair and the curving darker eyelashes gave his handsome face the look of a mischievous angel in an Old Master.

An impression, George McCord reminded himself

with bitter resignation, that was totally erroneous. Devil would be more like it.

"It's no laughing matter," he said stiffly. He and his client's grandson rarely saw eye to eye, but he would have hoped that the letter from Cyberfuture would sober even the heedless, reckless last heir of the house of de Vouvray Ward.

"What, then?" Hal tossed the letter back onto the older man's desk. Mail from Cyberfuture routinely went to his grandfather's lawyer, and it was a mystery to him why old George had bothered to bring it up. "Did the old man tell you to show it to me?"

A politer man, George McCord reflected, would have used the verb "ask." Testily retrieving the letter, he laid it flat under his hand without looking at it again.

"He hasn't seen it. I naturally consulted you first."

"What's it got to do with me?"

"Well, for one thing, if I may be so blunt, it's your sperm."

Hal yawned luxuriously and stretched. One arm was encased in a plaster cast, and he winced as certain muscles flexed. "Sorry, George, we were working late last night in the lab."

"Any child born of this error will be, in effect, your own child," McCord continued.

"No, it won't, George," he corrected in a lazy voice, "it'll be a scion of the house of de Vouvray Ward. Isn't that why the old reprobate forced me to deposit sperm with this outfit of incompetents? It's got nothing to do with me."

"I was not aware of force being used."

"Sure you were. You were right there in his office

when he threatened to cut off my access to my own money unless I did it, weren't you?"

George naturally chose the easier point first. "Legally, of course, it is not your money."

"Legally, my grandfather is on a level with the family pirate. That money was my father's independent fortune," said Hal, showing his teeth, "and if he'd stuck around till I was born you know damned well the first thing he would have done would have been to sign the new will."

"But he did not. The old will left your mother a lifetime income and the bulk of his personal estate to your grandfather, who is entirely within his rights…"

Hal yawned again and looked at the watch on his good arm. "Can we get this meeting over with? I left my engineers working on something interesting. Anything else on the agenda? It's the end of the month. Aren't you supposed to drum the month-end figures into my head?"

It was another toll his grandfather exacted from him in exchange for the money: every Monday morning he came and sat here while George McCord outlined the company's position to him. It was the old man's still faintly beating hope that if his grandson was regularly forced to listen to a rundown of events in the corporation's life, he might one day decide he wanted a hand in running the place.

"I don't think," said McCord irritably, "that you have appreciated the gravity of the situation Cyberfuture's error has created."

"But you're about to convince me, right? All right, go ahead. It might be amusing, and I could use a laugh."

"I thought you said you'd had a good night and were working on something interesting." The lawyer couldn't prevent himself from showing interest, although he was under instructions not to discuss the work Hal Ward was doing.

"It's not the R&D, George. That's going fine, or it would be if we had enough money. Anytime I talk about my grandfather, I need a laugh afterward."

"Well, Cyberfuture's mistake is no laughing matter. Of course, they'll be suable," George said, looking on the bright side, "but the woman may be suing, as well, and it seems unlikely the company will have extensive assets."

"I can see why the woman would sue."

"Particularly as you're Rh negative."

Hal frowned. "What does that mean?"

"It's possible the baby's blood will be incompatible with that of the mother. If she hasn't been pregnant before, there will be no problem with this pregnancy, but it could cause trouble later. No doubt," the lawyer said cynically, "that is the only reason Cyberfuture has owned up to this mistake."

"So she's got reason. Why would *we* sue?"

"Surrogate parenting has meant changes and new interpretations of the law. In a few years, who knows what ruling the courts might make on some attempt by this child and his mother to claim against the de Vouvray Ward estate, or even Ward Petrochemical?"

Hal sat up at this, his eyebrows raised with the first real interest he had shown during this interview. "That's not what the letter says. It says they won't divulge my identity."

The lawyer smiled grimly, shook out a white hankie and polished his reading glasses. It was the first time he had ever seen Hal express any interest in the fortune, and the corporation, which he would one day, *if* he lived, inherit. Maybe he was waking up at last.

"Naturally Cyberfuture is putting the best possible face on it. If the woman pursues it, it may be that the courts will deem her entitled to know the donor's name."

"This kid—" Hal, his attention frowningly focused on the lawyer, indicated the letter lying on the desk "—might be legally entitled to a share of the estate?"

"As I said, the courts are increasingly difficult to predict on these matters."

Hal Ward let out a roar of delighted laughter, his head thrown back, all the tension leaving him as his body was flung back in the chair. Then he winced with pain.

"Shot himself in the foot!" he cried, clutching a hand against his side, where the lawyer knew he had suffered five—or was it six?—broken ribs. "The old bastard—maybe this'll teach him not to interfere in my life!"

"If your lifestyle were less dangerous and wild—" the lawyer began.

"My lifestyle be damned! It's the old man's obsession with dynasty that's the problem! What the hell does he care who inherits the money? He'll be dead! By God, George, I hope the kid's mother comes after him for half the cookie! With a little luck she'll want a seat on the board! How much trouble could she cause?"

"Too much," said McCord feelingly. "We'll have to take steps."

"You bet your life you will! The only question is, will the poor woman survive any steps The Two takes?"

The older man put his glasses back on his nose and stared at the younger one over them, but if the stern look was meant to quell his high spirits, it failed. Hal Ward was still alternately laughing and holding his strapped ribs.

"Your grandfather—" the lawyer began, somewhat pompously, because he disapproved of the grandson's use of the nickname that everybody used of Harlan de Vouvray Ward II behind his back. "The Two" for "The Second"; sometimes reduced to "TT". "Your grandfather has always been a most respectable and respected man of business."

Hal leaned back in his chair, still grinning. "Yeah, but the Ward blood, George! There's a long line of adventurers and con men stretching out behind us, guys who did what had to be done. I may be a throwback, but if TT has always been respectable, it's because nothing ever bit close to the bone, and you know it. But this will." His laughter rang out again. "Man, I can't wait to see his face when he hears about this one!"

"What did you say?" George McCord babbled. He stared at his employer, his face a blank of surprise. The sun glinted off the old man's silver-white hair, but there was no resemblance to an angel in *his* face. The thick, dark eyebrows, an inheritance from the French blood and the unmistakable hallmark of the de Vouvray Wards, were pulled into a permanent expression of frowning concentration, and the carved lines from nose to mouth did nothing to soften the impression of impatient intelligence and ruthless determination to get his own way.

"I said, I want that woman!" said Harlan de Vouvray Ward II emphatically. "I want her here, under my eye! You get her here, George."

The lawyer's eyes slid uneasily from side to side, as if someone might have entered the office behind him without his noticing. No one. "What woman?" he asked carefully.

"That one!" The old man waved impatiently at the letter in the lawyer's hand. "The one who's pregnant with my great-grandson!"

George McCord leaped involuntarily in his chair, like a rat in an electrified cage. "Harlan, are you nuts? How do—"

"I don't give a damn about the how! Kidnap her, if necessary! Just *get me that woman!*"

"Harlan, with all due respect, what the hell are you talking about?"

The old man glared at him. "I want that baby, George," he said, in a voice that brooked no argument. "He's my great-grandson, and I want him."

"It's illegal to try to buy a child," said the lawyer flatly.

"We won't have to buy the child. Go and tell that woman who we are. Tell her I want her to come here—"

"Tell her who you are? Harlan, if she sued, God alone knows how much she'd be awarded!"

The old man stared at him, and George McCord was quick to press his advantage. "The best we can—"

"Shut up, I'm thinking!" Harlan de Vouvray Ward II croaked in a voice suddenly gone hoarse. His thick eyebrows beetled together over his nose and he stared at a point in space just behind McCord's ear. The lawyer waited in silence for the fierce eyebrows to stop working.

The Two slapped his hand on his desk, making the other man jump.

"By *damn!*" he said triumphantly. "That's it! He can marry the girl!"

"Forget it."

"You fathered this child. Don't you think you owe the mother of your child a decent name?"

"*A*, I did not father this child, and if anyone owes her anything it's your incompetent friends at Cyberfuture. *B*, as I understand it, she already has a decent name. What's the woman's name, George? I'm sure you've managed to get it out of them by now." Hal spoke to the lawyer, but his gaze didn't leave his grandfather's face.

"Carlee Miller," the lawyer supplied.

"Miller. Perfectly decent name. Her husband's forebears used to grind flour in a mill, TT, which is a lot more decent than pillaging ships on the high seas like the Wards."

"Dammit," protested his grandfather. "Only one was a pirate. You make it sound like a family business! What about my French grandfather? He was—"

"One was a pirate, and one was hanged from Tyburn Tree as a highwayman, and the one that struck oil killed his mistress's husband in a duel and two others—"

"I know the stories, no need to repeat 'em," said his grandfather.

"Women don't lose their good names through being pregnant and unmarried anymore, TT, or have you been asleep for the past thirty years?" Hal continued, pressing his advantage.

"A woman who's pregnant would rather be married," the old man insisted. "A pregnant woman will always jump at marriage, as my French great-grandfather used to say."

"I wonder what experience gave him that insight."

"Pregnancy makes women want security. Marriage makes them feel secure."

"The answer is no."

TT heaved a noisy breath. "All right. All right, I didn't want to have to do it this way, I wanted to give you the free choice—" he ignored Hal's crack of laughter and went on "—but since you force my hand, here it is. You're going to marry this girl. You don't have to live with her, I'll put her up in the house with me. But marry her you will. You're going to give that child the legal right to the name de Vouvray Ward."

Hal was staring at the old man with narrowed, disbelieving eyes. "Well, you've finally done it. You've proved you're certifiable."

"I mean it. You marry her and you marry her fast."

"Or?" Hal prompted grimly.

"Or your funding for this damned car you're building is cut off completely as of the next time you ask for money."

Hal slammed to his feet. "This is an outrageous,

indecent proposal and you know it! You know damned well the money you're threatening to cut off is mine by right. Twenty-nine years ago when the will was read you promised my mother that if she didn't contest you'd act fairly over my father's money! She trusted you. You make the family pirate look like a choirboy!''

George McCord, looking from one to the other, realized that there was no time when the younger man resembled his grandfather so much as when they were both angry.

''I kept my word! You have always had an income appropriate to your station,'' said TT loudly.

''Not appropriate to the financing of the kind of research I'm working on! If you cut me off now—''

''Research? You call building a racing car research? A young man's fancy, that's all that is! Time you stopped all that dangerous nonsense and settled down to some real work! Get married, boy, it'll change your outlook on things. Dammit, I want to get out of harness. I don't want to die like an old workhorse!''

''Don't play the tragic old man card with me, Grandfather,'' advised Hal. ''You can shuck the harness whenever you like. Mike's panting to sit in your chair.''

''Mike's not family.''

''I've got a solution.''

The old man eyed him with suspicious hope.

''Suppose *you* get married and father a daughter, TT. Then you can marry her off to Mike and he'll be family.''

''By God, I'll cut your funding off next week!''

"Right," said Hal, capitulating suddenly. He was stiff with fury. "I give in. I'll get married. I'll marry whoever you want." He lifted a hand and pointed at his grandfather. "You find the woman, you explain the deal, and if you can get her to do it, I'll marry her, and you live with her."

"You can't expect a woman to—"

"That's my last offer," Hal cut across his grandfather's protest, his voice deep and grating and filled with angry contempt. "Take it or leave it."

He slammed out of the office so violently the windows rang.

2

Carlee Miller stood at her kitchen table looking out at the world. She had two views, one through the window beside the table and one through the door that stood open onto the backyard, where the afternoon sun was glinting on still-damp grass and a bird was singing of summer with full-throated ease.

She was thinking. Mostly she was thinking about the best laid plans of mice and women.

How had it all gone so wrong? All their perfect plans, Bryan's and hers, all dust. In so short a time her life had gone from being utterly happy and mapped out to being filled with grief and the unknown.

Two and a half years ago any one moment of her life had held an image of the whole, like a hologram. Walking up the aisle of Buck Falls United Church to where Bryan stood waiting for her, she could see it all: lots of children and then even more grandchildren, and Bryan beside her right through till sunset. Starting out in the little three-bedroom house they'd already bought, and then a move to a bigger place when they'd outgrown it. Their children growing up healthy and happy, with maybe someone famous among their number—a hockey player on an NHL team, for example, or a prime minister, or a great writer—but all of them happy and fulfilled even if nobody ever heard their names outside of Buck Falls, British Columbia.

They'd bought the house "in need of updating," because, as Bryan said, they'd rather have space than carpets for their money, and they could do it up themselves. The first time he'd fainted he'd been on the stepladder, papering a wall. It wasn't very long before they knew that what had made him faint would probably kill him very soon, unless he was one of the lucky ones.

"Of course you are," Carlee had promised. "Haven't we always been lucky? Meeting each other my first day of grade school—you don't get luckier than that."

But they would have to give up on that dream of a houseful of children. Even if he survived, the treatment would probably make Bryan sterile.

"We'll have us," Carlee said. "And we can adopt."

They hadn't gone on a honeymoon when they got married, because they'd wanted to spend the money on fixing up the house. So before he started treatment they decided to take Bryan's dream trip—driving down through the Rockies from Vancouver all the way to Baha, Mexico. Neither of them said aloud that Bryan's "trip of a lifetime" might be exactly that.

They first saw the Cyberfuture ad in a magazine in San Francisco, but the idea didn't gel for a hundred miles. Carlee couldn't figure out why it hadn't occurred to them before. Freeze some of Bryan's sperm!

And when he'd recovered, they could start their family....

He hadn't recovered. He was one of the many, not the few. After six months of being a bride, Carlee was a widow.

She'd got over the horrible, immediate pain of loss with time, but she'd always known that what she'd had with Bryan was the sort of once-in-a-lifetime thing that could never be repeated. Making up her mind that she would probably never want to marry again, Carlee had looked for ways to fill her life.

Teaching was a good start. She had always loved her work, and she'd be satisfied to make it her lifelong career. Maybe she'd go back to university later and move on to teach high school. But that wouldn't be enough, she knew. Carlee was too much of a homebody to think that career alone could make her happy.

Not much more than a year after Bryan died, both Carlee's parents were killed in an accident. Maybe it was that second unbearable loss that had pointed the way to her.

It had come to her out of the blue one day, as if on the wings of a song. She didn't have Bryan, but she could still have the baby they'd planned on. Or even babies.

It had taken some serious long-term planning, and a lot of saving. The insemination procedure had to be paid for, and the trip, and she had to plan for taking a whole year off work, and then a couple of years of part time, because she wasn't going to have a baby only to give it to some other woman to look after. And if she didn't have quite enough, her sister, Emma, a successful lawyer in Toronto, had promised that money would never be a problem. Emma would always be there.

And now here she was, pregnant by a stranger, whose Rh negative blood might cause a problem because she was Rh positive, and with no chance of ever having Bryan's baby because the lab had somehow destroyed all of Bryan's sample.

How could it all have changed so fast? How could it have gone so wrong? She hoped it was over now. What would she do if things kept on going wrong?

The doorbell rang.

"Mrs. Miller? Carlee Miller?"

"That's me."

"My name is George McCord. I wonder if I might have a few minutes of your time."

"If it's a religious thing, I'm—"

The man looked pained. "No, I'm not trying to sell you anything at all. What I have to say is rather private." He took out his wallet and fished out a business card. "May I come in?"

"Gee, I'm sorry," Carlee said, letting him inside. "But out here, you know, we get a lot of doorstep religion. And you're a complete stranger, so I just naturally…"

"Quite all right. I understand."

Carlee tensed with sudden nerves. He was an ordinary, graying man in a business suit, but who dressed like that in Buck Falls on a Saturday afternoon? Sneakers and jeans was the uniform here. She glanced at the card, but all it said was, "George McCord, Legal Affairs Administrator, Ward Petrochemical" and an address in California.

"Please have a seat. Can I get you a coffee or something?"

"Thank you, no."

He sat down on the chair she'd indicated. Carlee perched on the arm of the sofa opposite him. "So."

George McCord cleared his throat. "Mrs. Miller, I understand you have already been notified of the extraordinary error that took place at Cyberfuture Laboratories."

"I got a letter last week."

"It informed you that the fertilization that took place on May 15 was with sperm not your husband's?"

"Yes, it did. Are you from Cyberfuture?"

"No, Mrs. Miller. I represent the sperm donor."

"Oh." Carlee moved from her perch to sink down on the sofa. Her eyes, very blue now, gazed at him. "How did you get my name and address? They told me they would keep it confidential."

"I'm sure you know there are always ways."

"What way, exactly, did you use?"

He coughed and shifted uncomfortably. "My client now has a controlling interest in Cyberfuture Laboratories."

Carlee felt alarm buzz along her spine. "Why? What do you want?"

"Mrs. Miller, am I to understand that you intend to continue this pregnancy?"

She touched her stomach in a reflex gesture of protection. "Yes, I do," she said firmly.

"Have you sought legal advice on this matter, Mrs. Miller?"

"You mean about suing Cyberfuture?"

"And related matters."

"My sister is a lawyer with a very big firm." Instinct made her not tell him that Emma lived and practiced three thousand miles away.

"Would you prefer to have her present at this interview?"

She fixed him with a look. "Look, your client's worried over nothing. I won't be bringing a paternity suit or anything. If you want me to sign a release, I will."

"As it happens, my client is a man of some substance."

"What do you mean, substance? He's rich?"

"This word is not inappropriate."

Carlee laughed. "I don't believe it! I get the wrong sperm, and it turns out it belongs to some American millionaire who can buy a whole company to get one name? Is this a joke?"

"It is not a joke, I assure you."

"What's his name?"

"Harlan de Vouvray Ward II."

Carlee went off in another peal of laughter.

"Harlan de Vouvray Ward II?"

George McCord looked faintly gratified. "If you already know of him that makes my—"

"There's a *person* named Harlan de Vouvray Ward II?"

"I assure you there is," he said stiffly. "Mr. de Vouvray Ward can well afford to undertake the expense of the child's upbringing."

She stared at him. "Well, if that's an offer, it's very kind of him. But I've got everything I need, Mr. McCord."

"An old established family in the town of Cantabria, California."

"Look, where I come from, he who pays the piper calls the tune. I'll do without your client's money, thanks all the same."

"Perhaps you would not object to listening to my client's story."

"It really won't make any difference, Mr. McCord."

"My client is approaching his eightieth birthday—my dear Mrs. Miller, what is the matter?"

"Eighty?" she repeated. Carlee felt sick. This, somehow, had been her worst fear. "I'm pregnant with the sperm of an eighty-year-old man? It shouldn't be allowed! What if it's not healthy? My husband was only twenty-four!"

"Mrs. Miller, please relax. My client is not the sperm donor."

"A minute ago you said he was." Carlee got to her feet, facing him, her hair ruffling spontaneously. "What's going on here? Who are you?"

"My client's grandson is the sperm donor," he assured her hastily, waving his hands as if to quell a riot. "Please, Mrs. Miller, we'll never get anywhere like this."

She eyed him for a moment. He looked uncomfortable and harassed, but not dangerous. "All right." She sat down again.

"Mr. de Vouvray Ward had the misfortune to lose his only son at a very early age. A few months after the son's death, his grandson was born. This child was and is the only heir to a considerable fortune and an old and honorable name."

"And he's my baby's—the sperm donor? What's his name?"

"Harlan de Vouvray Ward IV."

Carlee rolled her eyes.

"Naturally my client took great pains in the raising of his grandson."

"I suppose he mollycoddled him and the kid rebelled," Carlee said practically.

"Well, *mollycoddled* is perhaps not the word," said George McCord, although he privately thought it was the best one he'd heard so far. "But *rebelled* certainly is."

"Does he do drugs?" she demanded sharply.

"I beg your pardon?"

"This boy who rebelled. Does he do drugs? Because the baby—"

"No. He races cars."

"Really?"

"Last year he won the Grand Prix twice." There was a note of unconscious pride in the lawyer's tone.

"That's all right!" she said admiringly. She didn't think the baby would mind inheriting that kind of adventurousness.

"It is not all right with his grandfather. Two months ago he narrowly escaped death in an accident in the Argentina Grand Prix. It was not his first accident by any means, but he fully intends to go back to racing the moment he is able to do so."

"Well, if that's his life—how old is he?" Carlee asked, getting interested in spite of herself.

"He is approaching thirty. He has never married and seems to have no intention of doing so."

"What does he look like?" she asked, for something had suddenly brought home to her the fact that her baby would not inherit Bryan's looks, but those of this stranger who was being described to her.

"What?"

"The—the sperm donor. My husband was a good-looking man, not real handsome in that Hollywood way—my mom always said you can't trust a really handsome man—but still, any child of Bryan's would have…" She blinked, because the sun seemed to have gone bright.

"You need not worry. Your baby's father is an attractive young man, and the Ward constitution is hale and strong. He is also endowed with intelligence, though you wouldn't know it from his actions."

Carlee was beginning to feel for the guy. "You mean, he doesn't do exactly what his grandfather wants?" she asked dryly.

The lawyer ignored that. "He has never fathered a child. His occupation is high risk. My client lives in perpetual fear of his grandson dying without providing an heir."

Carlee went still as the pieces fell together. "I see." And she did. Suddenly she did not want to hear any more. "Well, thank you for telling me all this. Now, if you'll excuse me, I have things to do."

"He is extremely anxious to recognize this child you are carrying," said George McCord, as though she had not spoken.

She looked gravely at him a moment. George McCord shifted uncomfortably. "I can never have my husband's child now, the lab destroyed his entire sample by mistake. Did you know that?"

He cleared his throat. "We were informed of it."

"And all your client could think about was Enter the Brood Cow, right? It's an ill wind that blows nobody any good, is that what he said about it?"

It was close enough to make the lawyer extremely uncomfortable. "I assure you he feels for your own position. In fact, he is very anxious to be of assistance to you."

Carlee sighed. "Yeah, I'll just bet he is." She jumped up as she felt her stomach's warning protest. "I need something to eat. You want a cup of something?"

He followed her meekly into the kitchen and sat in silence as she bustled around.

"So what are you saying? Are you saying you want me to name The Fourth as the father on the birth certificate?" she asked a few minutes later, as he sat munching the delicious sandwiches she had conjured up and she ate carefully burned toast. George McCord, always susceptible to good food, could feel himself relaxing for the first time on this mission.

"Mrs. Miller, let me tell you right out. My client would like to propose that you come to the United States to live and bring the child up under his eye. He suggests that you and the child's father marry, in order to secure the absolute legitimacy of the child, but that you would live, not with his grandson, but with him.

"In return, he promises to look after your financial future very comfortably for the rest of your life. He will also send the child to the best schools and—in short, Harlan de Vouvray Ward II is prepared to groom your child as his heir and successor—both to the de Vouvray Ward estate and to his company,

Ward Petrochemical. Your child, Mrs. Miller, will be a multimillionaire.''

The silence stretched out as she stared at him, the piece of toast forgotten in her hand. "Are you crazy?" Carlee demanded at last.

"I assure you, I am perfectly in earnest," George McCord said unhappily. "It may sound unusual—"

"It sounds completely Wacko, Texas, if you want to know! Marry a guy I've never seen and live with his *grandfather?* I don't know what you consider normal down there, but up here in Canada we call that kind of thing twisted. I don't even know if I believe you're who you say you are anymore. Maybe you're just some weirdo from Cyberfuture who gets his jollies talking about sex to strangers. Or maybe you—"

"I have not talked about sex," McCord protested stiffly.

"So living with my would-be husband's grandfather, what *is* that talking about, exactly?"

George gasped in horror. "Nothing like what you're thinking! You've got entirely the wrong impression! It would be a strictly busin—strictly impersonal arrangement. Just so you have somewhere comfortable to live while awaiting the baby."

"Maybe I didn't make it clear I'm comfortable where I am," Carlee said. Her stomach was heaving and she hastily nibbled more toast. "The answer is no."

George cleared his throat. "My client is extremely anxious to—"

"Mr. McCord, your client, it seems to me, is anxious to make everybody do exactly what *he* wants. Let me tell you something. I'm not happy about having a baby who's half Harlan IV instead of half my husband, Bryan, but I'm doing my best to get over the unhappiness caused by somebody else's mistake and just have a *baby*.''

''I'm sure that's very—''

''I've given you my answer, and I think you should take it, okay?'' She got up. ''Now, if you don't mind, I have things to do.''

Politeness forced the lawyer to stand. ''Mrs. Miller, I feel you haven't given my client's suggestion any consideration whatever.''

She shrugged. ''There's nothing to consider.''

Ruthlessly leading him down the hall, she opened the door. He said desperately, ''Think of the advantages your child will have.''

Carlee eyed him with real disfavour, tossing her hair back. ''I'll give my child all the advantages he or she needs, thank you, right here in Buck Falls. The biggest advantage any child can have is a loving home, and we'll have that.''

''You can't have considered the inheritance. Your child will have an opportunity that very few—''

''It hasn't made Harlan de Whatsit IV happy.''

''Mrs. Miller, please give me another few minutes to put my case.''

She closed the door again and crossed her arms. ''I thought you said you weren't going to try to sell me anything.''

''Certainly not!''

''Well, you sound just like a vacuum cleaner sales-man I had in here a couple of weeks ago. He wouldn't go, either, until I'd looked at every single plastic attachment in his case and he'd sucked up half the Kleenex in the house.''

George McCord blinked at her.

''He scared the neighbor's cat, too, Pussum—she was sleeping under that chair and he sucked up her tail thinking it was a hair ball.''

''Well, I hope you don't think I'll scare the neighbor's cat,'' McCord said indignantly.

Carlee giggled. ''She doesn't come around much anymore.''

''Please, Mrs. Miller. May we sit down again, just for a few minutes, and discuss this in a little more depth?''

Carlee tilted her head. ''Look, Mr. McCord, I'm not interested, okay? If the baby's great-grandpa wants to visit and get to know the baby, that's fine, and in fifteen years, who knows? But I prefer to run my own life. Goodbye, Mr. McCord.''

3

"**I**s this Carlee Miller?" It was a nice male voice, low and resonant. A slight accent. American, probably, but she couldn't be sure on so little evidence.

"That's me," Carlee sang.

"This is Hal Ward, Mrs. Miller."

She waited, but there was no explanation.

"And what can I do for you, Mr. Ward?" she prompted.

"You don't recognize my name?"

"Not this time. Next time, maybe."

Hal groped for words. How could he describe himself? *The inadvertent father of your child? Your partner in the sperm bank foul-up?* "Well, I—our connection is a little difficult to describe right off like that. We both patronized a place called Cyberfuture one day last May, and you—"

"Are you Harlan de Vouvray Ward IV?" Carlee demanded, interrupting, which was a thing she taught her kids never to do.

"Hal Ward," he said firmly.

Carlee drew a fulminating breath. "I *wish* you guys would leave me alone! Dammit, I said no and I meant no! Understand?"

"Yup. That's about how I feel," the voice said mildly, and now the accent was clearly American. Funny how a voice could tell you so much about a person you'd never met. He sounded warm, funny and sexy, not at all the kind of voice she would have expected from a fast-living millionaire who raced cars.

"Mrs. Miller? You still there?"

She surfaced with a start. "What do you mean, that's how you feel?" she demanded suspiciously.

Her voice seemed familiar somehow, but he couldn't work out who it reminded him of. "I called to congratulate you on the way you stood up to the old ba—to my grandfather. Also to say I'm grateful. And I'm afraid it's my fault you had to take a stand. I didn't. I caved in."

"Oh-h-h," Carlee's voice caroled curiously. "Don't you *want* to marry me, then?"

"Nothing personal, I assure you."

She laughed. She had an easy, scratchy, infectious laugh, but when Hal discovered he was trying to put an image to her, he brought himself up short. The less personal this got, the better.

"But then, I don't understand. Why would you agree to it? Mr. McCord said you agreed."

"Blackmail," Hal told her briefly.

"Blackmail?"

"Strictly between you and me, my grandfather has the legal control of my money. If I want my money, and I do, I have to marry you."

"Golly!"

"Pardon me?"

"Nothing, I just said *golly*."

"I thought that was what you said. I just didn't believe it. You said *golly?*"

Carlee snickered helplessly, sounding even more like a kid. "Yeah, I know, but I teach grade six."

"Kids in grade six say golly? Not the way I hear it."

"Well, they do a bit of cussing here, too, sometimes, but it sure won't help matters if I start doing it, will it?"

"You're not in the classroom now, and I'm pushing thirty."

"You can't just change a habit once you get into it, Mr. Ward," she informed him.

"I guess not. So suppose you start calling me Hal right away? I'd hate for you to get into that Mr. Ward habit."

"But we won't be talking again."

Hal blinked in surprise. What did he think he was doing? "Nope. You're right. You got me."

"It's nothing personal, but I just don't think it would be a good idea."

"Well, just you stick to your guns and we won't have to talk again."

"Oh, you can count on that," said Carlee. "Goodbye, then."

He wasn't used to women dismissing him. Hell, he wasn't used to women not wanting to *marry* him. Perversely, he found he wanted to keep her talking, but that was pretty stupid.

"Goodbye," Hal said.

"Offer her a million or two up front."

"I assure you, Harlan, she is likely to take umbrage. Why don't we concentrate on getting Hal married to someone else, now that he's agreed in principle? Sharon Harlowe-Benton is a good prospect."

The Two shook his head impatiently. "'One is better than two you *will* have,'" he quoted.

George looked blank.

"That's what my grandfather Vincent used to say. It's the French for 'a bird in the hand is worth two in the bush,' George," he explained. "And he's right. It's Mrs. Miller we've got to concentrate on."

"You've got visiting rights, she's agreed to name Hal on the birth certificate. What more do you want?"

"She could disappear at any moment. Suppose the child needs urgent medical attention and she can't afford it?"

"Then no doubt she'll apply to you for funds."

"George, I want that child here under my eye."

"Carlee?"

Carlee recognized the deep, attractive male tones instantly. "You said you wouldn't call me again," she accused.

"There's something I thought you'd want to know," Hal responded meekly.

She heaved a sigh. "*Now* what?"

"He's not going to give up, Carlee."

She almost shrieked. "*Who's* not going to give up?" But of course she knew.

"Harlan de Vouvray Ward II, head of the See the Ward Dynasty Safely into the Future campaign."

"Look, I've got other problems, I can't take this," Carlee said. "A pregnant woman is—"

"Are you ill?" he demanded. He remembered that

there might be a problem because of his blood type. He didn't like the thought of it.

"Physically I'm fine. I'm just rattled because today I found out that my friend Anna got a job down east, and I'm going to have to find someone new to go to Lamaze classes with me."

"My grandfather would be delighted to oblige, I'm sure."

"Your grandfather can take a flying leap. What's the matter with that man? Do you know he hired a detective from Vancouver to snoop into my life? What'd he do that for?"

"How did you find out about it?"

"You think we get big-city strangers poking around asking nosy questions here, nobody does anything about it?" Carlee countered.

"Ahh," said Hal. She could hear that he was amused.

"Four people called me in a twenty-four-hour period to warn me what was going on. Joey and Matt have got big bikes—"

"Joey and Matt?"

"I teach Matt's little brother Hank. Joey and Matt aren't nearly as tough as they look. The two of them put on black leather and roared down into Vancouver and asked this detective who his client was. An American, he said. That's got to be your grandfather. What was he doing it for?"

"I take it he's not doing it anymore."

"What?"

"You're using the past tense."

"Oh, well, naturally they asked him politely to stop asking questions about me."

"Politely? You call that politely?"

Carlee frowned at the receiver, then put it back to her ear. "What do you mean?"

"Way I heard it, they mentioned a possible gang raid on his offices by a civic-minded group called The Devil's Riders in the middle of a dark and stormy night."

"What?" Carlee choked. "They told me they explained nicely that people in Buck Falls don't like stangers poking their noses into their lives." She gurgled into laughter. "And he agreed it wasn't a nice thing to do! That's what they said."

"I guess they didn't want to knock off your rose-colored glasses."

"Well, I knew it couldn't be as neat as that, but— *The Devil's Riders?*"

"Better have a little chat with them about manners," he advised.

"Are you kidding? I never heard what you just told me, that's all!"

"Why do I feel that you're being derelict in your duty to civilization?"

She ignored that. "So, your grandfather told you all that—he tell you what he was after with his snoop?"

"Well, he has found blackmail useful in the past, as I can attest. Probably he's developed a taste for it."

"Blackmail! Honest to God, what could I get up to in Buck Falls? Anyway, I'm a widow, what I do is my own business."

"Where there's life, there's hope," said Hal irrepressibly.

"If he doesn't cut it out, there won't *be* life, because I'll go down there and throttle him with my own hands."

"You really are a woman after my own heart," Hal said, with deep appreciation. "I can advance you the price of an air ticket if you happen to be a little short at the moment."

"And *then* he tried to buy the baby from me! Can you figure this guy?"

"Try and see it from his point of view," Hal advised, his lips twitching. He loved hearing her call Harlan de Vouvray Ward II "this guy." Nobody in Cantabria ever called him less than "Sir."

"A million dollars, if I give him the baby within twenty-four hours of giving birth!" Carlee exploded. "That's obscene!"

"Also illegal, I believe. What did you say?"

"I asked him if that was per pound, and if I ate a lot and had a big baby would the price go up."

Hal shouted with laughter. He hadn't heard *that* from the old man. "And how did he react?"

"He said that was his best offer, and the price would go down as the birth approached, so I should agree while the offer of a million was still good. What's the matter with your grandfather, anyway?"

"He loses his sense of humor when he's fixed on something. It's what makes him a successful businessman."

"Well, he's not going to be successful in this."

Hal coughed apologetically. "That's what I called about."

Carlee's heart sank. "I forgot you said there was something new he was up to."

"He's going to institute proceedings to get joint custody of the child on my behalf."

She wailed on a long, falling note. "Can't you stop him?"

"Carlee, I am so close to a breakthrough in my research. I have got to have money *now*. If I give up now I lose two of the best engineers in the country to a competitor."

"Your research?" she demanded.

"I'm—designing a car."

"A car! What kind of a car?"

He didn't answer.

"I heard you're a Grand Prix winner. Are you talking about building a car for the Grand Prix?"

"Ah...yeah."

"That's a car race!" she stormed. "This is your baby's future!"

There was a silence. Both of them listened to what she'd just said. Both decided to pretend it hadn't been said.

Then he said, "I can give you the money to take off for parts unknown. I can support you there in reasonable comfort indefinitely."

"Leave Buck Falls?" she cried.

"There must be other nice small towns in Canada."

"But I'd be all by myself! I've lived here all my life! My neighbors are my friends!"

"I know it sounds selfish, but believe me, the timing of this thing couldn't be worse as far as I'm concerned. All I need is another six months, less if the luck goes our way. A year at the outside. We're sure of that. Then I'll be free. I won't need his money. *My* money,'' he amended.

"No?" she asked disbelievingly. "You'll win the championship with your new car and then it'll be out of your system?"

"At the very least I'll be able to take the design to other people and get the funding I need. All I need is a year at the outside. By the time your baby's six months old you can move back to Buck Falls."

"Thanks for nothing."

"Carlee, I can't fight him now. Give me a year, and I'll get him off your back."

"You don't understand that this year is crucial. I'm pregnant, Hal! Suppose he finds me in one town, do I run to another? What happens with my medical care and my Lamaze classes? I just keep changing doctors? You're asking me to spend my pregnancy as a fugitive."

"Right," he said. There was a long pause as he took it in. "Yeah, you're right. I didn't think of those things."

She said, softening, "Anyway, why should he win a bid for joint custody? All you are is a mistaken sperm donor. No judge would listen to him."

"That will depend very much on where the hearing takes place."

"Why wouldn't it be in Vancouver?"

"My grandfather, if it hasn't sunk in yet, is a master string puller. The sperm was technically resident in California."

"Sperm can have a place of *residence?*"

"There's a first time for everything, especially in

the reproduction business. He might be able to get the case heard here. He knows a lot of people."

"And owns most of them, I suppose!" she snapped, not that it was Hal she was furious with. "Damn him, what *right* does he have to do this to me?"

Hal said nothing.

"And where would I find the money even to attend the hearing, let alone hire a lawyer? I'm still paying off my last trip down there."

"You've been here recently?"

"How do you think I got pregnant?"

"Well, I can pay your legal expenses for you to fight it, anyway."

Carlee could feel her heart thumping, felt nausea brush the pit of her stomach. Absently she reached for the cold burned toast she kept handy. "You know how stressful a lawsuit like this is going to be? Somebody trying to take away my baby even before it's born? Pregnant women shouldn't be under this kind of stress, it's bad for the baby."

"It is?" He hadn't heard anything like that before. No reason why he should. Up till now pregnancy hadn't been an overriding concern with him; only avoiding it for his partners.

"The mother's state of mind during pregnancy is a big indicator in the health of the baby. The baby might be born with asthma or something if your grandfather does what you say!"

This worried him. Not that he felt any personal connection to the baby; he didn't feel it was his child or anything like that. But it wasn't Carlee's fault she was pregnant with the only de Vouvray Ward heir on the horizon and consequently his grandfather's prey.

"Look," said Hal, suddenly. "I know it's not what you want, but suppose we give in?"

"He really—what?" Carlee faltered in the middle of her fulminating speech.

"It's not what either of us wants. But—Carlee, suppose we give him what he wants? Suppose we get married?"

4

There was a moment's silence.

"The world's gone crazy all in the last five minutes, right? Pretty soon it'll happen to me," Carlee said faintly.

"You have to be crazy to put one over my grandfather," said Hal reasonably.

"I don't see how giving him exactly what he wants counts as putting one over him."

"That's not what we do. We *pretend* to give him what he wants, to disarm him."

"We fake getting married?"

"No, no."

"I think I'm lost already. I'm going to hang up now. I've got some hard thinking to do."

"Let's just look at it, Carlee," Hal said hastily. "We get married, and you come down here to live, as if permanently. On the strength of that I extort a large chunk of cash from TT for research purposes. The more I look at it, the more I like it."

"Where do you live?"

"I live in a small house on the estate. It used to be the estate manager's house a century ago. But you don't have to live with me. My grandfather inhabits the family mansion, and you'll live there."

"I have to live with a man you can't stop calling 'the old ba—'?" Carlee asked ironically.

"With a little luck you'll never see him. The place is big, and it's crawling with domestic staff. You won't lift a finger to cook, clean or anything else."

"Catch up on my reading, huh?"

"You'll also have access to the best medical care in the country."

"I want my baby to be born at home," Carlee said sharply, as if he had threatened her with a chrome operating table, bright lights and forceps. The thought of unnecessary high-tech interference in a natural process terrified her. If the old man could force her to—

"You can have that. You can give birth in the ocean surrounded by dolphins if you want, I hear that's the latest thing."

"You have dolphins?"

"I can get them. Believe me when I say that whatever money can buy, you can have."

"You're really seriously rich, huh?"

"Not me," he said.

"Okay, so there's me and a baby that now has your name—*last* name, I'm not saddling anybody with the name Harlan—and what then?"

"A year from when you arrive, you and the baby go home. If not before."

"You promise to divorce me and give me sole custody after one year?"

"You have my word. If the current lines of research are as promising as it seems right now, even earlier."

"What if they aren't? What if you don't get what you want after a year?"

"I will stop asking my grandfather to fund the R&D, whatever happens," he said.

Carlee felt she was being sucked against her will into seeing this scheme as a possibility. She said, a little desperately, "And suppose your grandfather threatened to pull the financial plug on you altogether if you didn't go after custody of the baby when I left? I mean, you're giving in to his demands *now* for money, what's going to change?"

"I am not dependent on him for the ordinary necessities of life."

"What can you do? Get a job and live like an ordinary person?" Carlee asked disbelievingly.

There was a short, pregnant silence. "It's not beyond the realm of possibility, Carlee. I do have an engineering degree."

"Oh, sorry! I thought you'd spent your life having a good time."

Hal laughed. "That, too. But when I was born my grandfather settled a certain amount of my father's money on me, and there's nothing he can do to revoke that. The interest is a good income, there's just not enough for running a research and development program on fu—on a car."

The more she talked to him, the less he was like the image she had of a rich playboy. She began to wonder what Harlan de Vouvray Ward IV looked like. There must be some reason why they couldn't find some other woman to have his children.

Maybe the lawyer had lied. "Attractive" covered a lot of ground. Carlee had found an old picture of

Hal Ward's first Grand Prix win, but it had only shown a guy in a silver jumpsuit with champagne being poured over his head by another guy in a silver jumpsuit. You couldn't see his features.

Not that his looks would affect her, one way or the other. If she'd been really bothered, she could probably have gone to a newspaper library in Vancouver and looked him up in some American paper.

"So if you give up your research, you're immune to pressure from your grandfather."

"That's right," agreed Hal.

"He wouldn't be able to force you to let him fight for custody of my baby?" she pressed.

"No. And let me remind you that once we're married, that baby will be in line to inherit a substantial part of the family goodies eventually, even if he doesn't get Ward Petrochemical. In fact—" he suddenly got an idea "—I'll tell TT you've agreed to marry me in return for a reasonable sum irrevocably settled on the baby. Then you'll have that whatever happens."

"He'll think I've given in to his bribery," Carlee protested.

"Never mind what he thinks. He'll find out the truth soon enough. A year is like two weeks to a guy his age."

"What happens if I say no?"

"Then I'll do my best to stop him going after you, Carlee, but the chances are he'll keep on coming till he's got what he wants."

"Which is, my baby." Carlee drew a deep breath and blew it audibly out. She wasn't sure why Hal's suggestion had gone from being totally ridiculous to almost…feasible.

"I have to think about this," she said. Maybe if she got off the phone common sense would return.

"When you get to know my grandfather," Hal said with a smile in his voice, "you'll learn that when it comes to women, he always quotes one authority."

"Really?" Carlee said, bridling a little at that *when.*

"My French great-great-grandfather. And you know what he used to say?"

"What did he used to say?"

"'A woman who considers is already lost.'"

The noise of the rotors faltered and died, and as the dust settled she could see someone striding toward the helicopter in the bright sun. Her eyes widened. Was this the man the lawyer had called *attractive,* the man whose looks she'd worried about passing on to her baby?

The door beside her opened. "Carlee? Hi. I'm Hal," he said, in a voice she recognized.

A mass of fine, lightly curling, gold-tipped hair that shone clean and silky in the sun fell over his forehead and down behind his ears to his collar. His eyes were green, with long dark lashes that were spiky with amusement, inviting her to laugh at the world with him. Above, strongly marked eyebrows, a broad, clear forehead; below, prominent cheekbones, a wide smile with straight upper lip and curving lower one and a strong jaw, firm chin.

For *attractive* read *looks to die for.*

His body looked "hale and strong" all right, in the

loose green khaki trousers and brightly patterned cotton shirt open over a strong, smooth neck. He was neatly built, muscular without overdoing it. He wore a plaster cast on his left forearm, and on his little finger, a simple pewter-coloured ring.

She'd heard that everyone in California was beautiful, a thing she hadn't believed till now. But he was really *too* handsome, Carlee told herself. A man shouldn't be that good-looking. "Handsome men can't be trusted," her mother had always said, and in the absence of solid experience to the contrary, Carlee would take her word for it.

"Hi," she said guardedly, but it was impossible not to return that easy smile. Suddenly her eyes fell to the cast on his arm and she frowned.

Hal's grin widened. "Yeah, I had a funny feeling!" he said. "We've met before."

"You were there!" she said in amazement, remembering. They began to laugh together, but for her it was the laughter of relief. She didn't know *why* it should make such a difference to think that they'd actually met on the day she got pregnant, but it did. "Your face was so bruised I don't think I'd have recognized you without the cast. How are you feeling now?"

"Just fine."

When they shook hands, Carlee was surprised to feel calluses. She'd always figured playboys had soft hands. But maybe driving did that.

"Thanks for coming to meet me. I didn't know what I was going to do if you didn't turn up," she said with a grateful, confiding smile. She sounded as if he were her only friend in a confusing world, and the moment she heard that note in her own voice she understood what her mother meant about handsome men.

"Well—" she continued, in a completely different tone, "I guess I'd have found my way."

Now, a funny thing happened to Hal just then. When he heard that "Oh, my savior!" stuff coming from her, he was instantly put on his guard, because her knight in shining armor he wasn't, especially not if it meant going up against The Two for her, and the sooner she learned that the better. But he'd barely had time for the thought when she withdrew.

It was as though someone soft had stumbled and fallen against him, and then got back on her feet before he could react. Clearly he didn't have to bother with any warning; the message was very clear that Carlee didn't intend to depend on him.

The funny thing was the flicker of regret he felt. Hal couldn't figure out any reason for it, so he simply forgot it.

Cantabria Airport wasn't very big; it mostly served the private jets and helicopters of the rich, of whom the community had more than its fair share. In the small car park Hal led her to a low-slung red sports car.

As he set her small carry-on bag in the trunk, Carlee said cheerfully, "I was wondering why you sent my luggage in by cab! There's not much room in there, is there?"

Hal Ward glanced down at her out of the corner of his eye, an amused smile tilting his mouth, and Carlee felt her own mouth smile. "What?" she demanded. "What did I say?"

Hal only shook his head. He wondered if she was the only woman on the continent between fifteen and forty whose breathing didn't alter when she saw this car. The only one he'd met, for sure.

"You want me to drive?" she asked, and Hal glanced at her in blank surprise. First time they'd met, and she was asking to drive his Maserati?

"I mean, it must hurt your arm, doesn't it? Is that from your accident?"

"Yeah, it is, but no, it doesn't hurt me to drive," he said. Which was true most of the time.

She opened her window the moment she got inside, so he didn't bother with the air-conditioning. After a minute he decided to go the long way, driving several miles in the wrong direction to get to the highway interchange. He put his foot down on the short, straight stretch between the two interchanges and roared into the fast lane.

Beside him, Carlee heaved a satisfied sigh. So speed turned her on. Well, he met a lot of women like that.

"Boy, this is nice!" she exclaimed. "There's just something about palm trees lining a road, and that blue sky!—it's just not the same up north, even in summer. Do you live near the ocean?"

Hal laughed to himself. "De Vouvray House has just under a half mile of sea front," he said, lifting his foot from the gas and easing into the center lane.

"Oh, good. Buck Falls is practically right on the ocean, too. I don't think I could ever get used to not being by the water."

"It's high cliffs. There's no access."

"Just seeing it will be enough. And hearing it crash."

"How's your sister?"

She laughed. "Oh, Emma got used to the idea pretty quickly, once I made up my mind. She told me to tell you she's very handy with a—"

"Machete, if anything happens to hurt you," he filled in. Carlee looked at him in surprise.

"You were talking to Emma?"

"Let's say Emma was talking to me."

"She called you from Toronto? Now, what'd she do that for?"

"Maybe she thought you wouldn't pass on the message."

"Well, really! I can take care of myself, and Emma knows that perfectly well!"

Hal glanced at her sideways. She didn't really look as if she could, or at least, there was something about her that might make a man feel protective. Not him, he wasn't the protective type. But a lot of men would feel it, he thought.

"Any second thoughts after we decided?" he asked.

"You know what? I just made up my mind that this is going to be a long holiday. How long before we're there?"

"This route takes about twenty minutes." At this speed it did. Hal usually made it in sixteen.

It was a graceful, beautifully proportioned home from another era, set high above the town, deep in its own fenced acres at the apex of a sweeping, tree-lined drive. The car with her bags had preceded them through the massive gates, a fact Hal noted with wry amusement, and her luggage was disappearing inside the front door as they arrived.

Carlee naturally expected to follow it upstairs. It hadn't been that long a journey, but after a taxi, a plane, a helicopter and a sports car, she felt in need of a damp facecloth and five minutes to herself. Also, she had to use the bathroom.

To her surprise, Hal led her down a hall on the main floor, tapped on a door and took her straight in to meet his grandfather, who was working at home this afternoon in anticipation. The Two was on the phone when they entered, his left hand holding the receiver to his ear, his right punching at a computer keyboard. He lifted his right hand to summon them forward to the two chairs in front of his desk, and they both obediently sat.

"Right with you," said The Two. "No, that's fine, Mike," he said into the phone. "Just give me that last one again."

Hal watched Carlee watch The Two with a certain compassionate amusement. His grandfather was impressive, with his craggy, tanned face and his enviably thick white hair and the sense of personal power that emanated from him. But there was no doubt that he was deliberately keeping Carlee waiting, as a means of subduing her for the future, and Hal watched to see how she would take it.

During the long five minutes that followed, she grew increasingly fidgety, and then, just as Harlan was finally putting down the phone, she got to her feet and moved to the door. Hal politely got up and followed her.

"I have to pee," she said softly, making an apologetic face.

Hal nodded and led her out of the room, up the central staircase and along the hall toward the room that he knew had been prepared for her.

"It's just one of those embarrassing things. Since being pregnant I can't hold it," Carlee told him.

"No problem," he assured her. "This is your room—there's an ensuite bath. Will you be able to find your way back to the office?"

"Oh, sure."

"I'll see you down there, then."

When he got back to his grandfather's office, the old man was waiting. "Where is she?" he demanded irritably when Hal came in alone.

"She needed the bathroom. She'll be back."

Twenty minutes later—twenty minutes that The Two spent fuming and pretending to work and Hal mostly spent grinning down at a car magazine—there was a soft knock at the door, followed by Carlee's second entrance. She had changed her clothes, Hal noted, and put her hair up. Her eyelashes were sparkling as if she'd had a shower.

"Hi!" she said cheerfully. "Since you were busy I thought I might as well freshen up a little. It's been a long trip, and I was kinda hot. Hope I wasn't too long."

"Quite all right," said Harlan de Vouvray Ward II in subdued annoyance. "I instructed Hal to bring you straight in to see me because I'm pressed for time, but there's no real problem.''

Carlee smiled generously and guilelessly at him. "You're forgiven," she said.

Forgiveness implies fault. Hal was pretty sure no one had had the nerve to forgive the old man for at least forty years. He had to suck in his cheeks to keep from laughing aloud as Harlan de Vouvray Ward II's expressive eyebrows twitched with perturbation and astonishment.

From then on, Carlee felt, everything was just a constant whirl of impressions and events. Sometimes it seemed as if that twenty minutes with Hal in the car was the last time she had had leisure to catch her breath. That first meeting with Hal's grandfather; being shown around the stately old-world mansion that nevertheless had every modern gadget, from closed-circuit security cameras to a Jacuzzi; having her bags unpacked by the woman who introduced herself as Carlee's personal maid; signing a million papers, including bank and credit card forms and, of course, a prenuptial agreement; visiting the de Vouvray Ward family doctor for a lot of blood tests; the rush of license applications and other formalities that had to be got through before the marriage could take place—all of these happened in an unreal haze. The only time she felt like herself was when she talked to Emma by phone.

At Emma's insistence, her firm was faxed a copy of the prenuptial agreement, and the best brains of Barton Bate Faddon were brought to bear on it. For

three days faxes hummed back and forth between Toronto and Cantabria, and at the end Emma said,
"They say they've got you a very sweet deal, compared to what other women are signing. It sure looks
good to me."

But the only clause that Carlee cared about was the
one that said the agreement did not in any way limit,
define or curtail the future rights of any child or children of the union.

The Two wasn't taking any chances with either of
the engaged pair changing their minds; he rushed everything. Five crazy days after Carlee's arrival, suddenly there she was walking through the doors of the
small Cantabria church—which had presided over
every marriage, christening and death amongst the de
Vouvray Wards since it had been built a hundred
years ago—to be married to a man she'd only met
once.

For it had to be said, Hal had abandoned her to her
fate. He'd delivered her to her doom, and left her
there.

Hal was in the church, talking to the minister near
the altar. He looked very handsome in a cream linen
suit and a green shirt that made his eyes a deeper
green, and she started smiling as soon as she saw him.

She was amazed at how relieved she was to see
him, as if he were an oasis of life in the desert of
cold impersonality she'd been experiencing. Hal
might be wild and reckless, but at least he was *human*,
and right now he looked like her savior.

Of course that was just pregnancy emotions, but it
wasn't just pregnancy emotions that had her suddenly,

desperately wondering what on earth she was doing. *I can't go through with this,* she thought wildly as she and George McCord and The Two strode unceremoniously down the central aisle. But the minister patted Hal's arm and turned to greet her with a smile, and all the doors on other choices seemed closed. Her heartbeat quickened suffocatingly.

"Hi," Hal said softly, as she came to stand beside him.

"Hi," she whispered back. She thought suddenly, *Mom was wrong. Hal's handsome, but I can trust him. You can tell by looking he's a man of his word.* And that seemed to make it all right.

"Now, who has the ring?" said the minister, opening his book to begin.

"Ring?" rasped The Two irritably. It was the one thing that had slipped through his dragnet of arrangements. "George, ring?"

This was unfair, and he knew it. George sputtered a denial. Hal, meanwhile, was laughing.

"I see Carlee is wearing a ring on her right hand," said Reverend Bill Pearson cheerfully. "Perhaps we can use that."

Carlee had remembered there should be a ring, not that she'd thought of reminding anyone. This morning, with a little whisper of apology to Bryan, she had moved her wedding band to her right hand. "This is the ring Bryan gave me!" she protested now, only just stopping herself saying *my husband.* Even so the minister looked at her curiously.

"Never mind that!" The Two ordered irascibly.

"It's just for the ceremony. We'll get you a replacement."

Carlee clenched her hand and drew it against her body, covering the fist protectively with her left hand. She gazed calmly at the old man. "No," she said, not rebelliously, but plain, flat, unarguable.

Suddenly Hal didn't feel like laughing. He was looking at Carlee, and he could see what he hadn't noticed immediately—that she had very carefully *not* dressed for a wedding. Her blue suit was not soft or romantic, but neat, almost businesslike. Her long soft hair was dragged ruthlessly back against her scalp and folded into a large chignon. Small silver studs were her only jewelry. No corsage, no hat.

Looking at her, he could almost visualize how she had dressed for her wedding with Bryan Miller. Her hair loose, a flowing, romantic white dress...pink flowers, probably. She was trying to keep that memory separate, maybe even sacred, by dressing absolutely differently now. And now The Two was trying to force her to use her wedding ring for this sacrilegious travesty of a loving commitment.

Hal wouldn't have thought he'd feel it, but he did. She pulled on his heart.

"Dammit, woman—!" the Two was saying, while the minister feebly expostulated that they could do without a ring.

"TT, you can't railroad over *every* decent feeling you meet in the world," Hal said, and while his grandfather was sputtering over the injustice of that, he turned to the minister. "My engineering ring will do for now."

He slipped the plain pewter band off his little finger and onto the minister's open book while Carlee threw him a look that would have melted stone.

"Right," said Hal. Whoever Bryan had been, he was pretty sure Carlee had been wasted on him, but the torch she was carrying was her own business. "Let's get married."

5

When they came out of the church, the unseasonable clouds that had been gathering earlier had darkened. At the curb sat the two de Vouvray Ward cars, in open defiance of the town's parking restrictions, not a ticket in sight. Hal's Maserati was right in front of the steps. A little farther along, under a heavy oak, sat his grandfather's limousine.

"Right," said The Two. "I suppose you'll be wanting to get back to your lab, Hal. Or the track. We'll take Carlee along to George's office. There's some papers she'll have to sign."

Hal frowned. "I thought she'd already signed every paper there was, including a contract with the devil. What else is there?"

Harlan de Vouvray Ward II gazed at his grandson impatiently. "A will, of course! No point getting her to sign that till the wedding was a done thing. You don't want half your assets disappearing up to Canada somewhere if something happens to Carlee while she's intestate!"

"*What?*" shouted Hal.

"It's just a formality," George assured him hastily.

The Two was unruffled. "You, too. George has

drafted your will up. You can drop in and sign that anytime over the next week or two, isn't that right, George?''

"No hurry," said McCord.

"Or you can come back with us now, if you have the time," said his grandfather, not without irony.

They had descended the church steps and were standing by the low sports car. Hal leaned down to open the passenger door.

"I'm afraid Carlee and I have more important things to do this afternoon," he said. She felt his hand at her waist silently urging her to the car.

Suppressing a grin, Carlee sank quickly down onto the passenger seat, and, waving a hand at the two astonished older men, swung her legs neatly in and closed the door.

Hal, meanwhile, having moved quickly around the car, was sliding into the driver's seat.

"Where are you going? Where are you taking her?" The Two demanded loudly.

"To buy a wedding ring, TT! Thought you'd approve!" Hal shouted.

The Two shouted again, but whatever he said was lost in the engine's triumphant roar.

Carlee was laughing for the first time in five days. "Oh, that was wonderful to behold!" She chuckled. "Thank you! Sign my will, of all things! On my wedding day! Hasn't he got any—"

"None at all," said Hal, wondering what the hell had possessed him back there on the sidewalk. Too late to turn back now.

"What kind of rock do you want?"

"*Rock?*"

"In your ring."

"Oh! In a wedding ring? A stone?"

"In your engagement ring."

"Good golly, what for?" she said blankly. "All I need is a simple gold band."

Which only made him more determined, God alone knew why. Hal flashed her a grin. "You're new around here, aren't you, ma'am?" he said, in the voice of a man trying to pick up a woman in a bar.

"How'd you guess?" she responded in pretend amazement.

"Wasn't difficult. Not many women around these parts question the need for precious stones," he said. "How about sapphires, to go with those eyes?"

"My eyes aren't sapphire blue."

"If you wear sapphires, they will be."

Laughter bubbled up in her. "Boy, that feels good! I thought maybe I'd caught some disease that meant I'd never laugh again."

"You did. It's called TT-itis. Fortunately it only lasts as long as you're in my grandfather's presence."

"I notice you didn't tell me this before you married me," she accused.

"You might have been immune," he defended himself. "Some people are."

"How many?" she demanded suspiciously.

"The percentage is low," he admitted.

"Low?"

"We haven't had a statistical sample large enough to discover the actual ratio. But we're talking parts per million."

She couldn't come up with anything more than another gust of rippling laughter in response to that, so she said, "*Who* is your French great-great-grandfather he's always quoting?"

"Vincent de Vouvray. One of the French de Vouvray cousins who came on a visit and married a de Vouvray Ward heiress back in 1885. He took the family name."

"What's so special about him?"

"Nothing. He was an aristocratic layabout who considered himself a philosopher. The Two was his favorite grandson, apparently. His wisdom on women fell on fertile ground."

"Vincent," said Carlee. "Is that who you're named after?" His full name, she had discovered this morning, to her horrified admiration, was "Harlan Vincent de Vouvray Ward IV," she recited, shaking her head. "No wonder you cut it down to seven letters!"

Hal laughed and pulled over in front of an ostentatiously expensive jeweler's facade. "That's the one. Here we are."

"My gosh," Carlee said, looking in the window.

"'Gosh,'" he repeated thoughtfully. "Is that a special Canadian expression?"

Carlee bit her lip and glanced over at him. "Now, cut that out! I told you it's because of my grade sixes!"

A two-carat diamond and sapphire cluster and one gold band later, they were eating lunch in a quiet restaurant that Hal never frequented. "It sure is some ring," Carlee said with a grin. They were sitting in an upstairs window, and the sun kept glinting through the tinted glass and catching the diamond.

Without thinking, Hal lifted her other hand, where

the plain gold band from the man called Bryan rested against her finger.

"Your husband never gave you an engagement ring?"

"Oh, he did. It was really pretty, I loved it. It got stolen one day when I was taking a swim class for one of the other teachers."

"And you never replaced it."

"By that time, Bryan was ill. The insurance paid up, but—there was just always something else to do with the money. And then afterward—well, if it wasn't something *he* bought for me, what did it matter?"

"I'm sorry," said Hal, kicking himself for having raised the subject that had turned her contagious laughter into glistening eyes and a trembling smile.

"Oh, that's all right. It's more than two years now. I'm over it, really, except when I think about it unexpectedly."

"You never met anyone else?"

"No." Carlee shook her head. "I know I won't, you know? We just had something so special. It could never be repeated."

"That's a pretty empty life you're planning for yourself."

She smiled. "No, because I'll have the baby."

"Right," said Hal. "I was forgetting the baby." For the first time he got the whole picture clearly: a woman who was still burning incense at the shrine of her dead husband was going to have his, Hal's, baby, as a memorial to that husband. His grandfather, on the other hand, was hoping to raise that same child as a memorial to the de Vouvray Wards.

And there was Hal, firmly in the middle.

Suddenly he had the sinking feeling that this thing was a recipe for disaster.

"Boy, I needed that!" said Tom Hayes with deep physical appreciation, wiping his dripping face with the towel that hung around his neck.

Hal was sweating, too. The two friends had just given each other a workout on the squash court, something that had been pretty much a weekly ritual since high school days. It was Hal's first game since the cast came off his arm, so the game had been less furious than usual.

As they walked toward the club's showers, the two healthy male animals were watched with a certain amount of female interest, but there was one pair of eyes that held something a little different than interest.

"Hi, Sharon," Hal said as he passed a thin, lean-muscled, raven-haired woman in tennis gear. She had one foot up on a bench beside another woman and was tying her lace. "Morning, Tess."

Tessa Clark looked at him with a grin. "Hal," she said. But Sharon hadn't heard his greeting. Tossing his squash racket into his other hand, Hal stopped beside her and put his arm around her as she straightened.

"Hi," he said again. "You free for lunch?"

She always was, of course, but today she gave a little start of surprise as she turned. "Oh, Harlan," said Sharon Harlowe-Benton, with a composure that was very far from her usual effusive response. "Lunch? Today?" She looked at him as though they'd met maybe three times in their lives and she disapproved of him. "No, I'm busy, thanks."

Hal blinked against the wave of pure, ice-cold hostility that emanated from her. He dropped his arm, saluted her casually with his squash racket, said, "Another time," and he and Tom continued on to the showers.

"Hoo, boy!" said Tom, when they were out of earshot. "My eyelashes are all froze up. What the hell have you done there, Hal?"

Hal was frowning in perplexity. "Nothing I can think of. I haven't seen her for a couple of weeks, but there's nothing unusual about that."

"No maybe about it," said Tom appreciatively.

"I'm starving. How are you fixed for lunch?" asked Hal, getting into the shower and lathering his hair vigorously.

"Sorry, not today! We're taking Ellie out for a picnic, and Daddy promised very firmly to be home in good time."

Fortunately, when he came out of the shower room, Hal saw Maddie walking past, alone and clearly at a loose end. "Maddie! Lunch?" he called.

Maddie Stonewald stopped in her tracks, looked Hal up and down and then smiled. Her luscious lips parted. "Drop dead," she said conversationally, and moved on.

Hal hung around at the bar for a few minutes, but no particular male friends of his turned up, and the women who would normally have jumped at the chance to lunch with Hal Ward were all busy.

People just didn't lunch alone on Sunday at the Cantabria County Country Club. They came to see and be seen, to talk and meet friends, and they did those things over lunch. But the lunch was incidental, excellent as the food always was. No one came here just *to eat*.

So Hal, whose only decent meal of the week was his Sunday lunch at the club, and who was ravenously hungry, bewildered by his new outcast status, went home to make himself a sandwich.

"But I'm not *used* to doing nothing!" Carlee exploded. "It's boring!"

TT gazed at her in amazement. "Go shopping, woman. Get your hair done. You've got a credit card for every fancy-priced boutique in town. As Hal's great-great-grandfather used to say, 'Women take shopping seriously because it is the business of their life.'"

"Hal's great-great-grandfather didn't live far into in the twentieth century, I understand. I've been shopping, thanks. And I had my hair trimmed already."

"Do it again. Around here women go to the hairdresser three times a week!"

Carlee looked steadily at him. "No," she said. "I want to do something useful."

"Well, you can't invade Sara's kitchen whenever you choose and demand to take over. Sara's a very fine cook and I'm damned if I'll lose her."

"Sara's a plain, boring cook. Why can't I do a little cooking on her day off?"

"You've just heard the under-cook say Sunday's his day to shine. Now, Carlee, I won't have the kitchen put into chaos because you want to cook up a meal now and then. Why don't you take up pottery?

Ella keeps a little pottery workshop. She won't mind if you use it in her absence.''

Hal's mother was in France, and Carlee already knew it was typical of the old man to assume that other people's feelings accorded exactly with what he himself wanted.

"How do you know she won't mind?'' she demanded rudely. "By what I can see, you've never considered anything except your own convenience since the day you were born!''

The thick eyebrows drew together. "Why would she mind? She's not here.''

"What you mean, TT, is, why would she mind when it would make your life easier if she didn't?'' Carlee pointed out ruthlessly. "I wouldn't use my mother-in-law's pottery workshop on your say-so, even if I wanted to, which I don't! I don't know the first thing about throwing clay, except I wish I had some in my hand right now!''

"You're right,'' The Two said abruptly. "It might not be safe for you to be breathing in clay dust in your condition. You never know what—''

He was talking to the air. Carlee had slammed out of the room.

"Carlee! Hi there!''

The low-slung red car pulled to a stop a few yards away on the lane that led through the estate to the house where Hal lived. Carlee, who had been furiously striding nowhere, moved through the trees toward him.

"You!'' she said.

"Hey, don't look at me like that! What's the matter?"

She took a deep breath. "I'm just remembering that you're the one who got me into this!"

He nodded in instant understanding. "Trouble with TT?"

"What is it with that man? How has he got through life without realizing that he's not alone in a world of toy soldiers all put here for his convenience and entertainment?"

"Just a knack he has."

"I'd like to clip him upside the ear!"

"I love it when you talk mean."

Carlee's mouth twitched into a smile, and her mood suddenly lifted. Just looking at Hal made her feel better.

"It's not that I mind a bit of leisure, but cooking *is* my leisure!" she said. "I don't see why I can't do some cooking *sometime!* And I'm bored with only eating plain American cooking, too! I like a little variety in my diet!"

"You can cook?" Hal asked, going right to the central issue.

"It's my favorite hobby, but Sara doesn't want anyone muscling in on her territory, so that translates into me never being allowed near a stove."

"*I* have a stove," he said hopefully.

"What?"

"And I haven't had lunch."

Carlee gazed down into his upturned face as his pleading smile stretched wider. My, how the man had teeth! "You're on!" she said.

"Hop in." Hal leaned over to open the passenger

door as she dodged around the car, and a minute later he pulled to a stop again at his own front door.

"Where do you keep your food?" she asked five minutes later, from the doorway of the room where Hal was bent over a funny little working model of something. She had just been through every cupboard in the kitchen.

Hal looked up. "What do you need?"

"Well, more than a couple of tins of tuna and half a loaf of stale bread. I'm a cook, not a magician."

Hal's stomach growled hopefully. "Is that all there is? Make a list and I'll go to Monique's."

"Is that that gourmet food shop I noticed the other day? I'll go with you," Carlee said eagerly.

So there they were: newlyweds on their first shopping expedition together. Carlee walked down the aisle beside Hal, her pregnancy hormones whizzing contentedly through her blood and subconsciously telling her this was the right scenario.

"Are you allergic to anything?" she asked, hovering over the dairy cooler. She hadn't made any decisions yet on the lunch menu, but Hal's fridge was as empty as the shelves in the old-fashioned pantry.

"I don't think so."

She put butter, yogurt, milk and cream into the trolley under his astonished gaze.

"Won't we get arrested?" Hal asked.

Carlee, leaning over the cooler with her head full of possible recipes, glanced up at him.

"What?"

"All those animal fats. Aren't they contraband?"

She laughed that scratchy, infectious laugh he had first heard on the phone. He remembered suddenly that it had made him wonder what she looked like. He'd been a long way from imagining this scene then.

"All that stuff you hear is just a fad," she said comfortably. "Next year they'll be saying they made a mistake and it's polyunsaturates that are the danger. I just eat naturally. Additives are a problem, but this stuff's all from an organic farm, and they don't use plastic packaging."

Hal nodded. "What's on the menu?"

"Let's see what fresh vegetables they've got. But I figure you need a few supplies, anyway." She carefully examined the stock of cooking oils and chose a bottle labeled Extra Virgin Olive Oil. Cold Pressed.

Hal tried to imagine any of his girlfriends stocking his fridge for him. If they did, it wouldn't be with butter and cream: every woman he knew considered butter a dirty word. Sharon had bought a take-out sushi once.

"Hal! Hello!"

Speak of the devil, he thought, looking up to see Alexa Harlowe, Sharon's young stepmother, gazing at him with greedy interest and synthetic surprise. He doubted she ever shopped for food, so she must have followed them in here. "Hi, Alexa."

"We haven't seen you for ages." This was true in fact, if not in implication. Sharon hated her stepmother, and Hal had seen a good deal less of Alexa while he was dating Sharon than he had previously. So the implication that he wasn't seeing Alexa now because Sharon was angry with him was all eyewash. Turning to Carlee with a pleased smile she crooned, "And is this the new wife we've all been hearing about?"

Hal's expression solidified suddenly, like volcanic lava hitting a glacier. "Um...yeah, right," he said. "Ah, Carlee, this is Alexa Harlowe."

"Carlee! How do you do? I'm just delighted to meet you!" Alexa gushed, with convincing sincerity. "We hadn't heard your name, just that Hal had secretly gone and done the deed with a complete stranger! We're all thrilled! It seemed as though no one would ever catch him!"

Carlee smiled in a friendly way. "And instead he caught me," she said.

"Abso*lute*ly! I hear you're staying up at de Vouvray House. I guess you're waiting till Hal redecorates his place."

"Come on, Carlee," said Hal impatiently. "I'm ravenous. Sorry, Alexa, but I haven't had lunch yet."

"Sure, I understand! Look, why don't you come over for drinks tonight? Just the usual crowd."

"Another time, maybe."

Alexa twinkled both hands gaily and ran out, not having purchased anything. They could see her through the windows, jumping into a haphazardly parked bright green convertible that matched her contact lenses.

Carlee looked up at Hal out of the corner of her eye. "Why's she so pleased about you getting married?" she asked as they moved toward the bakery. Because, for all the woman's glittering falseness, that pleasure had rung true. "Two French sticks, please," she said to the assistant.

"Because I've been dating her stepdaughter," Hal said thoughtfully. This morning's scenes at the club suddenly were making sense. He hadn't once given thought to the fact that the news of his marriage would get out. And he'd been an idiot not to take into consideration the impact it might have on his social life. He had some fast talking to do, he could see that.

"And I don't suppose you date ten-year-olds," said Carlee, who immediately saw it all. "She married a guy twice her age, and she'd hate like hell for her stepdaughter to snaffle a bigger prize, is that what I hear?"

"I object to the term *snaffle*."

"Win."

"No one would call Harald Harlowe second prize. He's rich enough, and at least he controls his own wealth," Hal said with feeling. "And the way I heard it, the competition was fierce."

"Yeah, but you're rich *and* young. And gorgeous," she added with impersonal accuracy, inspecting the mounds of perfect vegetables in the fresh produce section. "Well, I don't think I like Alexa very much." She reached for a purple-black eggplant in peak condition. "Is she going to be your stepmother-in-law someday?"

Hal blinked in momentary confusion. "What? No!"

"What's your girlfriend's name?" She was adding plum tomatoes and fresh parsley and zucchini and lemons to the cart almost at random. Hal's mouth was seriously beginning to water.

"Sharon Harlowe-Benton, and as of this morning she's very much my ex-girlfriend."

Carlee giggled in astonishment. "You mean, you never *told* her?"

"I didn't think that far ahead. My stomach's growling. Can we get going?"

Carlee obediently moved on. "So there goes your social life?"

"There are always other fish in the sea," Hal said, with easy confidence.

They ate by the pool, and Hal stuffed himself. He hadn't tasted anything so delicious in years. She made a whole mess of little *tapas*-like dishes, from garlicky chicken to eggplant and tomato in olive oil, and he loved them all.

"Boy, where did you learn to cook like this?" he demanded, when first the edge and then the body had been taken off his hunger and he was eating just on taste alone.

"It's my main hobby. I take courses every summer, and usually one night a week in the winter. I've done Italian, Spanish, Indian, Middle Eastern, Russian, Greek and French so far. This summer I was going to do Polish. I love cooking. People warned me that I'd go off it now that I'm pregnant, but it hasn't happened so far."

"Dammit, I've only just found you, and now you're going to go off cooking? I don't live right!"

"I doubt if it'll happen. Most women stop feeling sick in the second trimester. That's at twelve weeks. I haven't had it so bad, and I don't suppose it'll get worse now. I've only got another couple of weeks to go."

"So the danger is over?" he said anxiously, making her laugh with his mock greed.

"What are you suggesting? You want me to cook

for you on a regular basis?'' teased Carlee, tilting her head and smiling.

"Would you?" Hal countered, blinking a little as the smile hit him.

"To get away from your grandfather? Anything," she said fervently, which wasn't the kind of reaction Hal was used to. He was generally appreciated more for his own sake. "How often?"

"I work long hours," he said. "But a good meal one night a week would go a long way. Tomorrow?" he added, just as Carlee offered, "Saturdays?"

"All right, Mondays," she said, laughing. Hal, meanwhile, soaked up the last of the garlic-tomato-something-else sauce with the last of the French bread, ate it, and surveyed the empty table with a sigh half yearning, half satisfaction with a job well done.

"What'll you cook tomorrow?" he asked.

6

When Hal laid down his tools in the workshop on Monday evening, everybody was suppressing grins. "Yeah, boss," Trev advised, "you get on home to the little woman."

Hal looked around to find his entire team eyeing him with approval. "What the hell?" he demanded, frowning.

"Congratulations, Hal," said another. "So you finally bought in."

"About time."

"Hear she's a real pretty little thing."

Hal stared at them, appalled, while the truth swept over him—his days were numbered. The marriage which he had so lightly entered into, the marriage which he had been determined would not shift his lifestyle an inch…was going to change his entire life. Everybody knew he was married, and if the team's sappy reaction now was any guide, everybody was imagining that he had married for love. Suddenly the reason for Sharon's anger became crystal clear.

He could see which way this thing was going: his sex life was blighted for the next year, or until the research was successful. If anything could give his work extra impetus, Hal thought, this was it.

For a while he toyed with the idea he might explain the situation in a limited way, maybe to Sharon. But two considerations prevented this. First, depending on how she took it, whatever he said might get around, and he couldn't predict what effect that might have on the way Carlee was treated by the community. And after all, he owed her some protection. She was here because he had asked her, and one way or another she was his wife. He couldn't just toss her to the wolves for his own sexual convenience.

Second, it was slowly dawning on him that every one of the women he had dated or who had indicated they would like to date him in the past had had their eye on marriage. With marriage out of the question, they were going to be a lot less interested in his charming company.

He was stuck with the charade. And when Carlee went home next year he was going to be a thing he'd never wanted to be—a type. Divorced man with one child. Things just wouldn't be the same.

It was in a mood of deep irritation against his grandfather for forcing this issue—and himself for so carelessly and thoughtlessly giving in—that he strode through the trees from the lab toward his own house and opened the gate in the hedge that surrounded the swimming pool.

A figure in a slim, black one-piece was streaming down the pool toward him in a ferocious crawl, and he stopped and watched the flashing, rounded arms in momentary admiration. When she reached the edge she did a tumble turn, and he saw her like an underwater arrow, shooting for the upper end. He walked along the side of the pool, and Carlee saw him as she swam, and stopped when she reached the top.

"Hi!" she said. She was gasping a little.

"Hi," Hal returned. "Shouldn't you be taking things easy? I mean, is it safe to swim so hard?"

"Don't you start!" Carlee erupted with a fury that took him aback, dragging herself out of the pool with a supple ease propelled by anger. "I have had it up to *here* with being told what's good for a woman in my condition!" She stood blazing at him.

"Your grandfather is a madman, and if you'd told me the truth about him, I would never have agreed to this in a hundred years! I'd rather be hiding out in *Elbow, Saskatchewan—*"

She made that sound like the Last Stop Before the End of the World, and Hal could believe it, a name like that.

"Elbow?" he repeated faintly, but Carlee was in full steam.

"—than listen to any more of his paranoid ravings! I am not made of porcelain, and neither is my baby! I am healthy and strong and fit and almost eleven weeks pregnant, and *I do not need to be wrapped in cotton wool for the duration!*"

"From where I sit, you don't need to be wrapped in anything at all," Hal said, eyeing the small, curvy figure with surprised appreciation. This was the first time he'd seen her not fully clothed, and there was something to be said for a woman who ate butter. It wasn't as though she was fat, everything seemed to belong exactly where it was. It was just that she didn't look like a starved cat.

"What?" Carlee demanded, shaking her head with incomprehension, and then she snorted and began to laugh.

"That's better," said Hal.

"Sorry," she said. "I shouldn't take it out on you, but that man is going to drive me crazy. I feel like a sacred brood cow. He watches every mouthful I eat, every move I make! I tell him the constant tension I feel because of him is worse for the baby than anything else, but he just can't seem to stop himself!"

Hal rubbed his neck. "Yeah, well, I know what that's like. I should have realized what he'd do if he got you here."

"Too late now," Carlee said.

She picked up a towel and briefly rubbed her face and then her hair, pulling it loose from the elastic ribbon to dry it. "But I told him today if he doesn't shut up I'm going back home." She tossed the towel and wrapped herself in a white terry cloth robe, flinging her hair back over her shoulders in graceful abandon.

Hal grinned appreciatively. "And what did he say to that?"

"He pointed out to me that the agreement I signed only pays me alimony if I stay till the baby's born." She headed into the house, drawing Hal in her wake. "I told him that I didn't want his dirty money and never have, and *he* said, then—" Inside the kitchen, she pulled open the oven. A delicious smell danced out into the room, and right there Hal went into a standing faint, sort of like a horse.

"Can you believe anyone would say a thing like that?" she was saying when he came to. She'd

checked whatever it was and closed the oven door
again and was reaching to adjust a control.

"I believe anything. What *is* that in there?"

"What?—oh, chicken."

"That's not chicken. That's chicken plus ambrosia
or something."

"It's a Mediterranean casserole. Honestly, haven't
you ever eaten before?"

"You've seen the kind of cook my grandfather
hires. Bad, plain cooking, all my life."

"But you must go to restaurants."

"It's not the same. What else are we having?"

"Nothing, until I go and change. Don't touch anything while I'm gone, okay? I changed in what looked
like a spare bedroom, is that okay?"

"It's fine. Can I pour you a drink?"

She threw him a curiously grateful look over her
shoulder. "Thank you. A glass of *wine* would be
nice."

He figured his grandfather probably frowned on her
drinking anything at all.

A couple of hours later they were sitting over the
remains of the best home-cooked meal he'd ever
eaten in all his life. Carlee was looking relaxed and
sleepy, all the lines of irritation gone from her face,
and he realized that she had really meant it when she
said that The Two's solicitude was making her tense.

Hal knew pretty well exactly what it was like, because his grandfather's passion to protect "the last of
his line" had ruled Hal's own life pretty much until
he left for college at age nineteen. He was making
her laugh with some of the details, but it had been

hell to live through, and Carlee seemed to understand that as even his mother never had.

"So what did the bodyguard do when you were swimming or something?"

"Sat on the dock and never took his eyes off me. If I went out too far he signaled me to come back in."

She rolled her eyes in sympathetic horror. "Where did he sleep? Across the doorstep of your cabin like an Arab slave?"

Hal shook his head. "Oh, no. He had a bunk right in the cabin. Two other kids, my bodyguard and me."

Her mouth was wide with shock.

"You must have *hated* it!"

He had. He didn't think of it much anymore, but he was suddenly remembering the humiliation of those summers at camp, year after year. No one had wanted to share a cabin with him, of course. Half the fun of summer camp was what you got up to after lights-out, playing tricks on the other cabins, sneaking off into the forest...not in Hal's cabin.

"Yeah, I guess I did," he said.

"No wonder you rebelled and started racing cars."

Hal frowned irritably. "Dammit, I did not rebel! I chose this life because I like it."

"Well, anyway, he's not doing that to my baby," she said, protectively patting her stomach, as if the child inside might have heard. "Making her feel centered out and paranoid about everything, or trying to turn him into a coward. This little de Vouvray Ward is going to have a nice, normal childhood, and take the normal risks of living."

Maybe it was that speech that did it, or maybe it

had been growing on him all evening, or even before that. Hal never knew exactly when and how he'd started feeling that he had to protect the child from his grandfather, or just when he started to realize that the longer Carlee was under TT's power the harder it would be to break his hold over the baby. All he knew was that the solution was obvious.

"Look," he said, "would you like to move in with me here? The place is big enough, and TT can hardly complain if my own wife comes to live with me."

There was a pause three heartbeats long, but it felt longer. Hal felt as if he'd crossed a chasm without looking, and only knew his danger now he was on the other side.

She was staring at him from wide, blue eyes, and suddenly the astonishment melted from her expression and she was smiling in sweet gratitude and relief. "Oh, Hal, would you mind? It would be perfect, but wouldn't I cramp your style?"

Not sure why he wasn't telling her she'd already done that, he shook his head. "No, I'm hardly ever here. I'd be on the road right now, except for this injury. I'll probably only see you at breakfast, if you're up. There are two spare bedrooms, as you saw. You can take your pick."

"It'll be a big change for you," Carlee warned worriedly. "Are you sure about this?"

He looked at her. "Believe me, I won't notice you're here," he said.

The thing was, he really believed what he was saying.

Thinking it over later, Carlee got scared. Hal was so good-looking, and worse, he always seemed to be

able to make her laugh. She wasn't falling for him—
she wouldn't do that, or at least not in any big way,
because after Bryan she knew she'd never be seriously in love again, but...suppose she got to like living with him? She didn't need a deck of Tarot cards
to see that Hal was irritated by the whole situation.
And whatever he *said,* she knew the arrangement was
affecting his social life.

It suddenly dawned on her that the worst thing
wouldn't be if The Two tried to stop her going home
at the end of the year. The worst thing would be...if
she herself didn't want to go.

She would have to be careful. Very, very careful.
She'd have to make sure she didn't allow any little
inroads that would make her feel she was losing
something when the time came to take her baby and
go home.

The Two was torn. It was clear he wanted to know
what the basis of this new relationship was, and hoped
it meant that Hal was going to settle down to marriage. On the other hand, he was afraid that Hal was
just doing this to thwart him and wouldn't take sufficient care of Carlee. After a short struggle his fears
got the upper hand. "I don't suppose you'll be hanging around the track..."

"In my condition," Carlee repeated mockingly
right along with him. "No, I won't be doing that.
What I'll be doing is living a normal life instead of
acting like Rapunzel in the castle."

TT frowned. "Rapunzel?"

"'Rapunzel, Rapunzel, let down thy hair,'" she

recited, and when he looked blank, "maybe that's your problem, you didn't get told enough fairy tales!"

This kind of tangential blow from her always caught TT off balance. Torn between challenging the idea that he had a problem, and querying the effect of a lack of *fairy tales*, of all things, on his life, he could only stare at her and demand, "What?"

"Fairy tales teach kids about life, you know. They describe psychological patterns. If you'd been told about the ugly old witch in Rapunzel, you wouldn't have to play that role in life—or at the very least you'd recognize that that was what you were doing and maybe be able to stop," she informed him kindly. "As it is, you just keep on playing it, over and over."

"Ugly old witch?" Harlan de Vouvray Ward II gazed at her in outraged fascination.

"She locked Rapunzel up in the tower to keep her safe, just the way you tried to do with Hal, and now me and my baby. But if your mother had only told you the story, you'd know already that you can't lock people up forever."

"You called TT an ugly old witch?" Hal said appreciatively, when she repeated the exchange to him that night over dinner. It had been less than an hour's work to pack and get her things shifted to his house, and then, with the help of one of the maids from the big house, she had cleaned and arranged the bedroom. Carlee was impatient of the restraints TT had placed on her, but it didn't blind her to ordinary common sense, and she knew better than to start humping furniture around on her own just because TT told her not to.

"Well, he is, isn't he?"

Tonight she had cooked Greek. They'd started with a *tsatsiki* dip with pita bread, and had moved on to a totally succulent *moussaka* and salad. If the truth were known, during the day at work Hal had forgotten that Carlee would be moving in. He'd dropped back to the house to pick up a floppy disk from his study, and in the kitchen Carlee had greeted him with, "Oh, great! I didn't know when to expect you, so I made something that would sort of keep if you were late. But here you are, right on time. Shall we eat by the pool? Twenty minutes okay?"

It just didn't seem possible after that to say he was on his way back to the lab. Anyway, the delicious smells of cooking drove everything else out of his head. Hal had changed into a swimsuit and done twenty laps while Carlee set the patio table. His injuries were on the mend.

Now he swallowed the last bite of *moussaka* and took a mouthful of white wine. "What is the story of 'Rapunzel,' anyway?"

"You mean, your mother never told you, either?"

"Maybe she did and I just don't remember the details."

Carlee licked her lips and took a sip of water. "Once upon a time there was a woman who started craving the cabbages that were growing in a nearby garden. Overcome by her constant entreaties, her husband at last went out in the dead of night to steal some of the cabbages for her. There he was discovered by the witch who owned the garden. In return for the man's life, and the right to gather as many cabbages as his wife wanted for the future, the witch demanded any child the couple might have. Since they had been wishing for a child for many years without success, the old man felt safe agreeing to this.''

"Dum de dum dum," Hal contributed, building the dramatic tension. Carlee laughed, her eyes sparkling merrily into his.

"Naturally the old man forgot all about his promise, until his wife gave birth to a daughter, and the old witch arrived to claim the baby. She took the child, whom she named Rapunzel, and locked her up in a tower that had no entrance except by a high window. The child grew up to be a very beautiful girl, with long golden hair. When the witch came to visit Rapunzel, she would call up to the window, 'Rapunzel, Rapunzel, let down thy hair,' and Rapunzel would drop her hair out the window to let the witch climb up.''

"I'm beginning to remember this," said Hal, nodding.

Carlee was pleased. "Your mother read it to you when you were little?"

The sun was setting in a blaze of color, and the sound of crickets and the faint gurgling of the pool were the only sounds on the soft evening air. In the distance, the sea shushed from time to time. He hadn't relaxed like this for a long time, Hal realized dimly. How different it was from eating in a restaurant, even a small intimate one. He leaned back in his chair and stretched his bare feet out, slipping his hands behind his head.

"I think I saw the film version. Wasn't this a Saturday morning cartoon?" She threw him a look, and he protested, "No, really. The prince comes in now, right? And *he* calls, 'Rapunzel, Rapunzel,' and she thinks it's the witch again and says, 'Boy, you're heavy today.'" He mimicked a high girl's voice.

"That's right."

"But I forget the end. What happens?"

"That depends on which version you read—or see. In the original, they fall in love, and the prince brings Rapunzel a bit of rope every day to weave into a ladder so she can escape, and when it's almost ready the witch discovers the ladder, cuts off Rapunzel's hair and nails it to the window, and when the prince calls, the witch lets down the hair. The prince climbs up and the witch cuts the hair so that he falls down and dies."

"Is that really the end?" Hal asked, shocked. "I thought fairy tales ended with everyone living happily ever after."

"It was a lesson about life, wasn't it? In the other version the prince rescues Rapunzel and kills the witch," she reassured him.

"I like that one better," said Hal.

Carlee smiled at him in sweet gratitude. "I guess you would," she said softly, and Hal suddenly saw the point. He had unconsciously been acting on the "prince rescues damsel in distress" model when he'd brought Carlee here.

He almost swore. This really wasn't like him. It wasn't like him at all.

7

He wasn't sure what woke him. It was unusual for him to wake in the night, and he lay listening and wondering if there was an intruder in the house.

For a long moment there was no sound except the night noises beyond his open window, but at last it came again, faintly. He still couldn't place what it was, but it was inside the house. Hal slipped naked out of bed and into the first thing that came to hand, which was the baggy cotton shorts he'd been wearing earlier tonight. He zipped the fly and buttoned the waistband as he made his quick, silent way to the door.

There was a faint band of light under Carlee's closed bedroom door, but when he cautiously opened it the room was empty. The quilt had been tossed back, and the bedside lamp was on. The window was wide open onto the night, and the curtains stirred gently in the wind.

His heart kicked into an accelerated rhythm and he moved quickly to the window, but the moonlight showed him nothing but grass and trees. He turned and went out and along the hall.

He heard the sound again, and saw the light around

the bathroom door, in the same second. His breath left him in a sigh of relief.

"Carlee?" He tapped gently on the door, and after a moment opened it and looked in. He was met by the sight of shapely, tanned legs, a neat butt encased in white cotton, and a back covered by a loose, dark blue T-shirt as she bent over the toilet waiting for another bout of sickness.

"Carlee," Hal said again. He stepped into the room and came up beside her, laying a hand gently between her shoulder blades. She glanced up at him just as her stomach convulsed again, and hurriedly turned back to the business at hand.

Suddenly all those nights with drinking buddies at college seemed to make sense as Hal discovered he knew what to do. He ran a washcloth under hot water, wrung it out and bent to wipe her forehead and face. Then he flushed the toilet.

"Thanks," she gasped. "Can you hold this?"

She held up her braid, which kept falling over her shoulder. Hal held it out of the way, while his other hand lay comfortingly across her back.

When the convulsion had passed, he wiped her face again, rinsed the glass that held her toothbrush beside the sink and filled it with cool water. "Here, rinse your mouth," he said.

Carlee gratefully did as she was told. Unconsciously, though he'd never done it for a college buddy, he began to rub her back. She felt cool to his touch. "All finished?" he asked.

She tentatively straightened up and smiled weakly at him. "I think so. Thank you."

"No problem. Is there anything I can get you?"

"I'd give my eyeteeth for a tomato sandwich."

"Coming right up," said Hal without a blink.

"Toasted white bread, no butter, with a little mayonnaise and a little lettuce," she added.

"Anything to drink?"

"Milk, please."

"You get back into bed, and it'll take me five minutes."

He heard the sound of her brushing her teeth as he went lightly down the stairs and into the kitchen, putting on lights as he went. He was good at sandwiches, it was all he ever made, so it was with an expert air that he slipped two slices of white bread into the toaster and located the mayonnaise in the fridge. He couldn't find any tomatoes there, and was on the point of going to get his car keys when he noticed a big blue and white bowl of them in the middle of the table.

It was just over five minutes later that he entered her room again bearing a tray. Carlee was in bed, propped up by pillows, reading by the light of a lamp.

"This is really nice of you," she said.

"S'alright," Hal assured her, setting the tray on her knees.

Carlee began wolfing down the sandwich in a way he hadn't seen her eat up till now. "Boy, I'm ravenous!" she declared between bites. "Oh, this is delicious, it's perfect, you've done everything just the way I like it."

"Good," said Hal.

"You're good at this. Have you got a lot of experience?"

"In a manner of speaking." He'd never thought of

engineering college as a training ground for marriage before, but he certainly felt comfortable now. Not that he could remember ever making a drunk roommate a tomato sandwich in the middle of the night, but the general scenario felt familiar.

As she drank her milk he suddenly noticed that the book she'd been reading was a book on pregnancy. He frowned as worry trickled through his mind.

"Have you seen Daniel Snyder yet? He's our family doc—''

She interrupted with a laugh. "With your grandfather running things? Are you kidding? I was down there my second day.''

"What did he say?''

"He took some blood tests, and since it's a first birth there's no problem with the Rh factor. I told him what kind of care I wanted, and he recommended someone who's into alternative birth. I've seen her once. That's one of the things your grandfather and I fought about. He wants high-tech care for me.''

"I remember I promised you you wouldn't have that.''

"And I won't." She shrugged. "TT can make appointments, but I don't have to keep them. There, that was delicious," she said, swallowing the last of the milk and setting the glass down. "Thank you.''

Hal took the tray and stood up, but not before he'd suppressed a funny impulse to kiss her, not passionately or anything, just kind of...friendly. But he guessed he'd better not.

"Good night," he said.

"Good night." Carlee snuggled down into her

pillows, and as he left the room, her bedside light flicked out.

She lay curled and comfortable in the darkness, full of wonder. He certainly was unexpected, Hal. The last thing she'd have imagined from a rich playboy who raced cars was the kind of caring she'd just experienced.

Sleepily she thought that Bryan would have done the same, if he had lived and this had been his baby. But Bryan had been her husband, he had loved her. She remembered how impatient Bryan had been with his own illness, how much he had hated his descent into dependence on her, and then on strangers, for his physical needs.

She had not disliked being cared for by Hal. She hadn't even minded him seeing her looking so dreadful—bent sweating over the toilet, face red. Her strongest reaction had been a feeling of human comfort. It was a lonely business being sick into a toilet at three in the morning in a strange place.

And then Hal had come to her rescue again and somehow it hadn't seemed such a strange place, and she hadn't felt lonely anymore. A little trickle of cold sweat slithered down Carlee's back, and her warm comfort abruptly died. She opened her eyes wide in the darkness, staring at nothing. It would be terrible if she started to imagine she was falling for Hal. Worse than terrible. She had always believed that what she felt for Bryan was so special she could never feel it for anyone else.

But she had never once considered that she might

feel something so completely different that it didn't seem the same emotion at all—and yet was still *love*.

Carlee was always down early, and in the morning, as he passed her open bedroom door, Hal did something he'd never done in his life before. He sneaked into the room and stealthily picked up the book on pregnancy that was still lying open on her bedside table.

She was reading a chapter entitled "Music and Your Baby," and he marked the page with a finger and flipped to the table of contents. "Establishing the Mental Connection," was one chapter title. "Touch" was another. Nothing on morning sickness, even in the index. Hal replaced the book and went out, feeling as guilty as if he'd read her letters.

"Is what happened normal?" he asked at breakfast, when she thanked him for his help during the night.

"Oh, sure," Carlee said. "I've had the same thing for weeks. It should stop soon, I'm almost at twelve weeks."

"I thought it was supposed to be *morning* sickness."

"Not everybody's the same. It takes different forms with different women. Mom told me once she was sick nights with me and Emma."

"Did you ask Dan Snyder about it?"

She looked at him. "If you're going to be just like your grandfather, Hal, I may as well go home today."

"I'm only showing human interest!"

But she did not want his human interest. If she started imagining it was more than it was—

"*And* suggesting that I'm not competent. I'll keep

you posted, and tell you if there's anything to worry about, if that's what you want, but you have to accept that I'm the one who's pregnant.''

"I don't think I've challenged that," he returned, a little annoyed that she should reject his offered involvement in this way.

But Carlee was fed up to the back teeth with Ward interference in her life. She'd made a huge mistake coming here. It must have been pregnancy hormones weakening her resolve, warping her judgment. And she was not going to compound matters by leaving herself open for hurt at the end of this.

"You're on the verge of it! I'm not a brood cow, Hal, I'm a woman of sound mind who has chosen to have a baby. You are incidental in this. Try to remember that except for a lab mistake you wouldn't know anything about this pregnancy. Believe me, I'd have got along without you."

For some reason that really pissed him off. "You didn't mind my interference last night!"

She softened and smiled at him, melting his anger. "No, I was really grateful. It's not everybody who can wipe your forehead when you're throwing up in the toilet. But you can't be boss of this operation, Hal, any more than your grandfather can."

He was not used to feeling his anger disappear like this, and he found it disconcerting. When he got into a rage with his grandfather, it usually consumed him, no matter whether he tried to control it or not. Usually he didn't try, just blew up at the old man and stormed out to cool down elsewhere.

"Okay," he said peaceably. "But I wish you'd

PLAY "LUCKY HE
AND GET . . .

★ **Exciting Silhouette Yours Truly™**

★ **PLUS a beautiful Cherub Magnet-**

THEN CONTINUE
LUCKY STREAK W
SWEETHEART OF

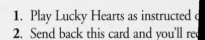

1. Play Lucky Hearts as instructed
2. Send back this card and you'll re
   Yours Truly™ novels. These book
   each, but they are yours to keep
3. There's no catch. You're under n
   We charge nothing — ZERO —
   And you don't have to make any
   purchases — not even one!
4. The fact is thousands of readers
   from the Silhouette Reader Serv
   of home delivery…they like get
   before they're available in stores
   prices!
5. We hope that after receiving yo
   remain a subscriber. But the ch
   or cancel, anytime at all! So wh
   invitation, with no risk of any

SILHOUETTE'S

With a coin— scratch off the silver card and check below to see what we have for you.

YES! I have scratched off the silver card. Please send me all the free books and gift for which I qualify. I understand that I am under no obligation to purchase any books, as explained on the back and on the opposite page.

201 CIS CCPE **(U-SIL-YT-11/97)**

NAME

ADDRESS   APT.

CITY   STATE   ZIP

Twenty-one gets you 4 free books, and a free Cherub Magnet

Twenty gets you 4 free books

Nineteen gets you 3 free books

Eighteen gets you 2 free books

Offer limited to one per household and not valid to current Silhouette Yours Truly™ subscribers. All orders subject to approval.

© 1990 HARLEQUIN ENTERPRISES LIMITED.   **PRINTED IN U.S.A.**

DETACH AND MAIL CARD TODAY

THE SILHOUETTE READER SERVICE™– HERE'S HOW IT WORKS:

Accepting free books places you under no obligation to buy anything. You may keep the books and gift and return the shipping statement marked "cancel". If you do not cancel, about a month later we'll send you 4 additional novels, and bill you just $2.69 each plus 25¢ delivery per book and applicable sales tax, if any.* That's the complete price–and compared to cover prices of $3.50 each–quite a bargain! You may cancel at any time, but if you choose to continue, every other month we'll send you 4 more books, which you may either purchase at the discount price…or return to us and cancel your subscription.

*Terms and prices subject to change without notice. Sales tax applicable in N.Y.

If offer card is missing, write to: Silhouette Reader Service, 3010 Walden Ave, P.O. Box 1867, Buffalo, NY 14240-1867

BUSINESS REPLY MAIL

FIRST-CLASS MAIL   PERMIT NO. 717   BUFFALO, NY

POSTAGE WILL BE PAID BY ADDRESSEE

SILHOUETTE READER SERVICE
3010 WALDEN AVE
PO BOX 1867
BUFFALO NY 14240-9952

NO POSTAGE
NECESSARY
IF MAILED
IN THE
UNITED STATES

leave your door open at nights, so if you need me, I'll hear.''

She smiled again. "Thank you, I'll do that.''

After that, as though he were tuned to her, Hal found himself waking the moment the bathroom door opened. By the third time, he began to feel like a real expert. "Tomato sandwich?" he asked when she was back in bed.

"Would you mind making some tomato soup instead?" said Carlee. "With some dry toast?"

"Soup coming up!" he said bravely, though his stomach quavered.

"Really burn the toast, please, Hal."

"*Burn* the toast?"

"I want black crispy bits."

He was pretty sure he'd heard that charred toast was bad for the heart or something, but he went out with a nod. He knew better than to argue with a pregnancy craving—though just *how* he knew that he couldn't have said—and besides, he had deeper problems to contend with just at the moment.

Soup. He'd never made soup in his life. He'd never even *watched* someone make soup. All he knew was it came out of a can.

The pantry was solidly stocked, he saw—for the first time since he'd moved into this house. Usually he was lucky to find a tin of tuna he'd forgotten. He ran his glance curiously over the supplies on the warped, ancient shelves. A jar of sun-dried tomatoes caught his startled eye—certainly he'd eaten sun-dried tomatoes in restaurants, but it had never before occurred to him that you could buy a supply of them like this, presumably to use in cooking.

"Coarse Bulgur," he read on another label, and on another, "Capers Preserved in Salt." What the heck did she do with this stuff? Was it all for pregnancy cravings? He hoped fervently she would never ask him for coarse bulgur or preserved capers: he wouldn't have any idea how to go about cooking them. Unless she wanted them straight up in a sandwich.

There was a shelf of more spices than he knew existed. He'd never seen anything more exotic than paprika in Sara's kitchen at the big house. He guessed this was what made the food Carlee cooked so delicious, yet he couldn't help eyeing the jars labeled "Garam Masala" and "Panchphoran" and "Ras el Hanout" with a certain suspicion. How could it be healthy for a pregnant woman to eat such weird things?

He found a small hoard of tins of Campbell's tomato soup on one shelf, and breathed a sigh of relief. This at least was ordinary. He'd never *made* Campbell's tomato soup, but he'd certainly *eaten* it. He was pretty sure all you had to do was read the label.

As he turned to go out, he put his hand up to the light switch and paused. The light switch had always been surrounded by a patch of dirtier gray against the dirty gray of the painted wall. Now the plate itself was cream colored, and the paint on the walls a kind of grubby pink. Hal looked up and saw the high-water mark two feet from the ceiling: she had scrubbed the shelves and the walls as high up as she could reach.

Hal had never noticed the dirt before, but he suffered a pang to think Carlee had had to scrub the place before she felt comfortable storing food in it. And he couldn't help noticing, now that it was forced on him, that even with the cleaning job the paintwork looked pretty revolting. The place hadn't been painted since he moved in, and probably a couple of years before that. He counted quickly and came up with 1988. It probably hadn't been painted since 1988.

In the kitchen again, he turned on a burner and hunted out a saucepan. Then he turned to the soup label. "Contents: Tomatoes, water, cream, spices…" His heart sank for a moment, but then he discovered "Directions. Empty contents"…right. He could manage this. He wasn't an engineer for nothing. First, though, he had to open the can.

The can opener wasn't in its usual place in the cutlery drawer, and he had a couple of panicked moments before he noticed the ceramic jar on the counter, full of utensils. He got the can open, but then a stink of burning assailed his nostrils. The saucepan he'd put on the burner was smoking.…

"Is it all right?" he asked anxiously ten minutes later.

Carlee spooned the soup greedily. "Delicious," she said.

"The soup's burned and the toast isn't," he pointed out guiltily. "I did it the other way around."

"That's okay," she said, pressing her spoon gently against the side of the bowl to flatten a glutinous lump.

"I'm sorry the soup's lumpy. I forgot the label said 'gradually' till it was too late."

Carlee smiled reassuringly. "Never mind. It's hot and wet."

"I never realized before what an art cooking is," Hal confided.

To his surprise, she began to laugh.

A couple of mornings later, feeling guiltier than a spy, Hal called Daniel Snyder from the lab.

"It's about Carlee, Dan," he said.

"Oh, yes. Congratulations, Hal. That's a very nice wife you've managed to find for yourself."

"Do you have to sound surprised?"

"Well, it was in the cards that a man like you wouldn't make such a good choice first crack out of the cannon," said Dan, who'd seen him through every illness and disease his grandfather had imagined he had since Hal was old enough to walk, and so felt he could talk turkey. "So, what did you want to ask about? Worrying about the pregnancy? You don't have to."

"Dan, she eats burned toast. I mean, really burned. Without butter," Hal burst out. He'd been appalled to see just what Carlee had meant by "the black crispy bits."

"Yes, some women do. Just leave her alone with her cravings unless they're not food."

"Not food?" Hal repeated stupidly.

"Some women crave coal in pregnancy. Or chalk. We don't really understand some of the pregnancy mechanisms. She's young and healthy, Hal. Stop worrying."

But Hal had a buildup of worries and couldn't hold them back. He quickly queried the 2 a.m. sickness and one or two other doubts, and Dan Snyder as quickly disposed of them.

"She's got shelves full of things like *Panchphoran* and *Garam masala*," Hal went on, reading from the list he'd hurriedly scribbled in the pantry when Carlee was elsewhere.

"What are they, cooking spices?" asked the doctor calmly. "Sounds like she makes curries. My wife makes curries."

"Yeah, she does." Hal momentarily forgot his worries in his enthusiasm. "We had lamb *dilpasand* the other night. Delicious! Better than at The Bengal Lancer, Dan," he said, naming the best Indian restaurant in three counties.

Hal wasn't consciously lying, it was just that he didn't realize that what made Carlee's curries seem extra delicious was the fact that he was eating them at home rather than in a public place. "We should have you around one night."

"You lucky dog. A great cook, too."

"Italian, too."

"Is she? I wouldn't have guessed."

"No, I mean, she cooks lasagna."

"Why are you worrying about the spices? Can't make a curry without *garam masala* any more than you can make a Bolognese without basil."

"Is *that* what's in curry?" He'd always figured it was curry powder. But he was only momentarily diverted. "Doc, is it safe for her to eat that kind of stuff? I mean, it's only Indian food, but she's pregnant."

There was a short pause. "Hal, think about it," Daniel advised. "Do you think Indian women stop eating curries when they're pregnant? What do you think they eat? Beefsteak and baked potato? The cow's sacred in India.''

"Oh," was all he could say.

"If Carlee is used to eating that kind of food on a regular basis, there's no reason to suppose it'll cause a problem in her pregnancy.''

"And she washed the walls. Should she be doing that?" Hal forged on.

"As long as she's not overdoing it, there shouldn't be a problem.''

"How do I find out if she's overdoing it?" Hal muttered hopelessly, half to himself. He was pretty sure the house was in a condition Carlee wouldn't consider clean. For a while he'd had a cleaner come in twice a month, but she'd quit about six months ago, and he hadn't got around to replacing her. Anyway, he remembered her saying she didn't do walls, so probably they hadn't been done for some time. If Carlee took it into her head to bring the place up to her own standards…

"For Chrissake, Hal, get a housekeeper. You're the richest man in town and your wife is scrubbing walls?"

"You're right," said Hal. "I'll do that. I'll do it right now."

8

Thus it was that, at eleven o'clock that morning, when Carlee was just leaving the house, she was startled to see a van come down the lane from the main road and pull up in front of the garage.

A woman with a clipboard, and two younger women and a young man who looked like university students, all in a uniform of shorts and polo shirt, jumped out. Both the van and the polo shirts carried the logo Spit and Polish.

"Hi!" said the woman with the clipboard. "I'm Elaine Mariner. We managed to get a team together right away."

"So I see," said Carlee.

"You're on your way out, I guess. That's okay, you can feel free, my employees are all bonded. We'll just get down to work."

Carlee pursed her mouth and looked at the woman for a long moment. Finally she said, "What exactly are you planning to do?"

Elaine Mariner consulted her clipboard. "Windows, walls, floors, upholstery and carpets, drapes, kitchen cupboards…that's on top of a regular cleaning, of course. Is there anything I've missed?"

"You're cleaners?"

The woman grinned awkwardly. "Established 1977. Isn't that what you ordered?"

"No."

She looked momentarily taken aback. "Oh, right! It was your husband I talked to! Mr. Ward," said Elaine, in the relieved voice of one who has solved a small mystery. "Gee, he didn't say anything about it being a surprise."

"And it's not even my birthday," said Carlee brightly.

She picked up on Carlee's irritation. The woman's smile faded. "Don't you want the work done?"

Now Carlee felt guilty. It wasn't Spit and Polish's fault that Hal was being an autocratic jerk, and the woman had clearly scrambled her forces to satisfy a customer at short notice. She blew out her breath.

"Oh, go ahead," she said, to Elaine Mariner's obvious relief. "Shall I leave you my key?"

Elaine shook her head. "Not unless you'll be returning after six o'clock. We clock out then. I figure we'll be here for two days, anyway."

"I'll see you later, then," said Carlee.

On the way into town in the car she stewed angrily for a few minutes. *The same old Ward interference,* she told herself. *Like grandfather, like grandson. Out of the frying pan into another frying pan.*

But in fairness it was Hal's house, and he had the right to have it cleaned without consulting her, she reminded herself after the first heat of fury had worn off. It wasn't his fault if she took it as a form of insult. Her problem was, pregnancy enhanced her naturally strong nesting instincts, so this felt like an invasion of her own territory. But objectively it was not her territory. Married to the owner or not, she was a temporary guest in his house. And it was in her own best interests to remember that.

Then she went to her first appointment.

"Your husband really is worrying quite unnecessarily," said Phoebe, the English midwife, at the end of her regular weekly assessment. "Everything's going absolutely beautifully."

"He is?" Carlee demanded. "I mean, yes, he is, but how do you know?"

"Dan Snyder and I *do* regularly compare notes, you know," the midwife said with a smile.

"Hal's been talking to Dr. Snyder?"

"I think he called to discuss some of his concerns. Perfectly natural, you know, from a first-time father. Men are much more likely than women to imagine that everything in pregnancy ought to go by the book."

Carlee took a steadying breath. "What exactly is Hal worrying about?"

The midwife laughed. "Burned toast, for one. I think Dan reassured him on that."

"So did I," Carlee said grimly. "What else?"

Phoebe gave her a you-know-these-insular-Americans kind of smile. "Outlandish spices have been discovered amongst your cookery items, Carlee."

"What?" Without really understanding why, Carlee was suddenly absolutely furious. It was a game to him, she told herself. He could be concerned now, but it was by no means a permanent concern. *Hal* could stop playing at any time. But if she relaxed her guard,

if she let this concern get to her…she might not be able to turn her feelings off so easily.

In fact, Hal's concern was no different than TT's. It was just a disguised bid for control.

Phoebe belatedly got the message. "Now, now," she said pacifically. "There's no point getting your knickers in a twist. It's just men, isn't it?"

"Not if I know it. From where I stand, it's just *Ward* men. What else is he asking about?"

Phoebe dropped her eyes. "I don't know, really. Dan didn't—"

"Yes, he did, and yes, you do, Phoebe," Carlee ruthlessly overrode her. "Please tell me."

"Apparently you did some rather energetic cleaning in the house," said Phoebe in a rush. "In fact, Carlee, he's perfectly right, it's better not to—"

Carlee sat through the friendly little lecture that followed with gritted teeth but every outward appearance of calm.

When Hal got home he could smell soap and bleach and polish, but the smell he was looking forward to was absent. There was no obvious odor of cooking.

In the upstairs hall, he bumped into Carlee just coming out of the bathroom, wrapped in a skimpy, frayed towel and smelling fresh and damp. Her wet hair was combed sleekly down over her back. The flesh of her shoulders and breasts was like newly ripe fruit, smooth and bursting with health.

Hal swallowed. "Hi."

"Hello," she said, and he saw that her normally

warm blue eyes were the color of ice on a lake. "Excuse me."

She turned away and walked to her bedroom, closing the door firmly behind her. Well, Dan had warned him this morning that pregnant women could get moody, but he was a little surprised it could happen so suddenly and for no reason. Maybe she was embarrassed being caught in a state of undress.

While he waited for her to dress, Hal wandered around downstairs, noticing the difference the cleaning had made...and the difference it hadn't made. No amount of shampoo could make the living room carpet seem anything other than old and worn, and in some places it had only made stains more noticeable. The clean windows meant the sun shone more revealingly on the faded wallpaper. And nothing could disguise the fact that the paintwork everywhere was cracked and chipped.

The dining room was in darkness, the table not laid, so he figured dinner would be a while yet.

But the kitchen table was laid. That was unusual at dinnertime; Carlee liked to make dinner an event. He lifted the lids on two saucepans sitting on the stove. Both held water that was just simmering. A cold frying pan rested on a third burner. On a plate beside the stove several rounds of meat were thawing.

"Ready for dinner?" Carlee said breezily, striding into the kitchen behind him. She'd dressed in cutoff jeans and a baggy shirt, her braided hair hanging down her back.

"Starving," Hal said appreciatively, pleased to be able to watch the magic she would now concoct. Usually it was mostly done by the time he got home.

She turned on the heat under the frying pan, brushed it with oil and dropped the thawed hamburger patties into it. Then she opened the freezer and pulled out something he'd never seen in her hands before: a bag of frozen peas. Ripping it open, she poured the contents into one of the pans as she turned up the heat in both burners, while Hal watched curiously, wondering what spin she could possibly put on this food to turn it into the feast she was sure to produce.

Then she went to the pantry and came back with a box of instant mashed potato flakes. Thinking he was hallucinating, Hal closed his eyes and looked again. Nope, he was right the first time. Instant mashed potatoes. He watched as she sprinkled a generous amount into the second pan of water, added milk and *margarine*, and stirred. She took it off the heat.

Boy, this was going to take some doing. This was worse even than anything Sara cooked for his grandfather. Hal was really surprised to see Carlee use commercial prepackaged food. Up till now he'd always imagined that everything she cooked was fresh, if not organic. He couldn't figure what she was going to make out of this.

"What are you making?" he asked at last.

"Mashed potatoes, peas and hamburgers," said Carlee. "Are you ready to sit down?"

Before he knew it, she'd expertly turned the potatoes and peas into bowls and slapped them on the kitchen table. She off-loaded the fried hamburger patties onto a separate platter and plonked it down.

Then she pulled out her chair. Hal was standing in the middle of the kitchen floor like the village idiot, watching her with bulging eyes. "Coming?" she prompted.

There was a bottle of ketchup in the middle of the table, with a plastic tub of margarine and the pepper and salt. Carlee sat down and forked a hamburger patty onto her plate as Hal shook himself and sat down.

Hal had eaten a lot of garbage food in his time, but just lately his taste buds had become acclimatized to flavor. He took an exploratory bite. The hamburger tasted like cooked cardboard, and the potatoes were hot, wet sawdust. The peas, thank God, were just peas. Carlee was eating cheerfully, smothering everything with ketchup, as if there was nothing out of the ordinary.

After all, it wasn't much worse than the hamburgers they sometimes ate at the lab when they'd worked past midnight and the only place that would deliver was the take-out near the drive-in, Hal told himself, and took another mouthful.

Suddenly light dawned. "I guess the house was too busy today for you to cook," Hal said.

Old ice eyes was back. "What do you mean? I just cooked."

"Yeah, but not—I mean, it's good, it's—" he cleared his throat "—it's not what you normally cook."

"It will be, from now on," she assured him sweetly.

Hal's white teeth flashed, and he laughed at the joke, his eyes glinting at her. "What?"

She didn't share the laughter. "Since all those

spices I used to use are so dangerous and un-American," she said levelly.

Sensing that he was under threat, Hal sobered. "What do you care about un-American, you're Canadian! What the hell is eating you, Carlee?" he demanded.

She set down her fork. "How *dare* you phone the doctor and check up on my actions, as if I were a child!"

He stared at her. "How did you find out?"

She didn't answer, merely flashed him a look.

"I was worried!" he said.

And how long will your concern last? She wanted to shout. She looked at those gold-lashed green eyes, darker now from emotion, and felt her danger. "You have no business being worried about me, and no business calling to ask my doctor questions. This pregnancy is none of your business!"

Hal was stung, and like anyone caught out, furious. "It's my baby, too, you know!" he shouted.

Carlee leaped to her feet. If in the end he wanted the baby, but not her, what would she do? "It is *not* your baby! It is *my* baby, and it has nothing to do with you or your grandfather or your clan or your damned dynasty or whatever you call it! Oh, I knew this would happen! I'd like to sue Cyberfuture into the bankruptcy courts for doing this to me!"

Hal was shocked at what he had just said. What the hell was he thinking of? Suddenly he began to wonder himself just what he'd thought he was doing when he phoned Snyder. He lifted both hands in a gesture of surrender.

"All right, all right!" he said. "You're right. It's

not my baby." Mollified but of course not really satisfied, Carlee sat down again. "But you're living here and I guess I can't help feeling concerned, and I don't see why it's such a sin to call Dan Snyder. I've known him all my life."

"I have told you before, I don't need your supervision!"

"Maybe you do, Carlee! You scrubbed the pantry walls, and that's not a good idea, is it?"

"If the deepest layers of dirt didn't show evidence from Noah's flood, maybe I wouldn't have had to scrub the walls!" she blazed. "Did you expect me to put food in there? It would probably have poisoned us!"

"You could have asked some of the servants from the house to come down to do the work."

"I wouldn't ask your grandfather for—"

"Why didn't you ask me? I'd have got you someone."

"Maybe, if I hadn't arrived home with all my shopping before I put the light on in the pantry, I would have asked you! As it was, it seemed easier just to wash the damn thing down."

"You shouldn't have risked it, though, should you?"

"Hal, for God's sake, some women have jobs as cleaners and they get through pregnancy!"

"Dan says in a first pregnancy there's a risk with things like that."

"Dan Snyder is not a midwife. Or even an obstetrician. He's just a doctor. It didn't put any strain on me to clean the pantry. I'm not Hercules, of course, but then, the pantry isn't the Augean stables. Almost, Hal, but not quite.''

"I'm an engineer, Carlee, not a Greek scholar."

"My grade *sixes* know about the 'Labours of Hercules'!" she snapped. It was a relief to be able to shout about something impersonal. "It's not exactly thesis level."

"Anyway, there's no river near enough. You'd have had to divert the swimming pool," Hal suggested, proving that his protest was so much eyewash, "and then what would you swim in?"

And just like that, the anger left her, and she was laughing. "Sorry!" she said. "But, honestly, Hal! Try to remember that if it hadn't been for a lab mistake you wouldn't know anything about my pregnancy and I'd be doing it myself." If only *she* could go on remembering that, she'd be okay.

"Yeah, but then you'd have had the whole of Buck Falls looking out for you," Hal said reasonably. "Can't you just look on me as a substitute, and take this as friendly caring?"

She smiled. He had a way of putting things in perspective. Why shouldn't she be able to stay at friendly caring and not want or expect more? "All right."

"Now, if it wouldn't be an insult to the chef..." Hal began tentatively.

"Yes?"

"How would you feel about eating out tonight?"

Since they were casually dressed, he drove down to the pizza place on the waterfront. There was a table for four outside at the water's edge, and the restaurant was hopping, but the waiter called Hal by name, unobtrusively slipped the Reserved placard into his pocket and seated them there.

"Boy, does everyone in this town recognize you?" Carlee said, picking up the menu.

"I went to high school with him," Hal disclaimed emphatically. "Don't get paranoid."

"High school? I thought your grandfather only let you go to the best private schools."

"That was elementary school. By the time high school came around we'd convinced him that Cantabria Heights High was academically sound and posed no more challenge to my morals and health than a private school would."

Carlee shook her head. "Uh-uh."

Hal grinned and looked enquiring.

"You think I lived with that man for two weeks without figuring out that nobody convinces him of anything?" she explained. "So how did you *really* get to go to the high school?"

He nodded. "I walked out of the private school on my sixteenth birthday, hitchhiked home and told TT that either I was going on the road, or I was going to my local high school. It's not easy to get a court order compelling a sixteen-year-old to attend high school, even for a man as powerful as TT."

She grinned at him in fellow feeling. "It must have been hard on him. I feel kind of sorry for him."

"Oh, TT's had his reverses."

"But just not lately?" she said gently.

Hal frowned. "What do you mean?"

"Well, if standing up to him worked when you were sixteen, how come you never did it again?"

Hal was irritated by the question, because the answer seemed so obvious. "Because he has control of my father's money."

Carlee shook her head lightly. "But you know what? There was something then, too. I mean, when you were sixteen. He probably had some hold on you then, he must have had. But you just—outbluffed him, didn't you?"

He was staring at her. "What are you trying to say, Carlee?"

She shook her head again. "I don't know, exactly. I guess—there's a point beyond which no one can really make you do what you don't want to. When you were sixteen you knew that. But somewhere along the line you forgot again."

Hal sat staring into the distance for a long minute, thinking about it. He looked up as the waiter returned with the wine he had ordered and, with a quick glance at the label, nodded. "Ger," he said, "I don't think you've met my wife. Carlee, this is an old friend. Gerry Maitland."

"Hi, Gerry."

"Carlee. Good to meet you. When I heard Harlan finally caved in at last my heart kinda went out to him, but I see I was worrying unnecessarily."

Carlee smiled.

"Gerry's a writer, Carlee."

"Oh, really?" She turned interested blue eyes on his friend, and Hal stifled a puff of irritation that it wasn't a look *he* saw often. "What do you write?"

"I've been working on a screenplay, but not so much just lately." Gerry grinned. "Hal, did you know Sheila had the baby?"

"I didn't hear! When?"

"Just two days ago. She's at home, everything went fine."

"A boy, right?"

"You've got a good memory. Yeah, well, they said a boy, and that's what he is." He was grinning proudly. "I know Sheila'd be pleased if you and Carlee would like to come around some night for a drink. She'd love to see you." He turned to Carlee. "Sheila and Hal and I were in the same grade in high school."

"I'd love to come and see the baby!" said Carlee, to whom a newborn baby was naturally an irresistible attraction. "Or—is Sheila well enough to go out? Could I cook you dinner? I haven't cooked for anybody but Hal for ages. And please bring the baby."

"I'll get Sheila to call you and arrange what's best," said Gerry. Then he took their orders.

"Do you mind?" she asked Hal, belatedly cautious, when he had gone.

"I haven't socialized with them as a couple much since they got married a few years ago, but there's no problem."

"Yes, there is," Carlee said. "What's the problem?"

He didn't tell her that his girlfriends had played a major role in his abandoning of the friendship. Sharon, for example, had always done her best to make Sheila and Gerry aware of their lack of money, and since Hal had gotten so busy at the lab he hadn't taken the trouble to force the issue. He saw Gerry often enough here.

"Did you and Sheila used to date?" Carlee pressed.

"Yeah, nothing serious, though. We were all dating each other."

Carlee understood that what he was trying not to say was that Sheila had maybe been carrying a little torch for Hal.

"Well, she has a baby now," she said comfortably.

"What does that mean?" he asked amusedly.

"I just think her world will have narrowed to the baby and his father, so that doesn't leave any room for dreaming about anybody else."

There was a funny look in Hal's eyes. "So, when your world narrows down, Carlee, who's going to be in it?"

Carlee's face lost its brooding smile. "Hal—"

"Hey, it's Hal!"

"Hal! Haven't seen you since the accident! How are you?" shouted a medley of voices, and then the table was surrounded by two very chic couples. It was the end of all intimate conversation.

Carlee wasn't sorry. She hadn't understood his question, but one thing she knew: she didn't want to have to think about the answer.

9

"**M**ore coffee?"

Hal nodded and watched absently as Carlee refilled his cup. Through sheer laziness, Hal had used to make himself instant in the morning, but Carlee made real Brazilian filter coffee and he certainly preferred the taste.

"We should buy a coffee maker," he observed, watching her ingenious method of pouring the coffee from the makeshift pot without getting the grounds into the cup. It was Saturday morning, and they had gotten up late.

"Actually..." Carlee began, then hesitated.

Hal looked up. "What?"

"Well, would you mind if I bought you some new pots and pans? All the coating is coming off your one and only frying pan, and none of the lids fit your pots."

"Why would I mind? You've got your own credit cards, haven't you? You don't have to ask me before you use them."

Carlee shrugged. "I don't want to interfere with your bachelor lifestyle too much," she said.

He wanted to tell her he could protect his own

damn bachelor lifestyle if necessary, but probably that wouldn't be fair. "If there's one thing an engineer understands, it's that a worker has the right to the tools he needs. You're a cook. The kitchen is your territory as long as you're here. Do what you like in it."

Carlee immediately pressed her advantage. "Can I buy a stove, too? Your oven—"

"You can rip the kitchen apart if you want."

She glanced around the old-fashioned room. It was very large and square with high ceilings, in the style of kitchens of fifty or a hundred years ago. Painted wainscotting reached halfway up the walls, black-and-white tiles covered the floor, and the cupboards were solid but discolored with age. An ancient, moss green enamel stove and fridge, the most up-to-date items in the place, sat against one wall.

"I wouldn't want to rip it apart," Carlee said hastily. "But a paint job would be nice. It reminds me of those family films in the forties. How come it was never done over?"

"The family's old estate manager lived here with his wife till they died ten years ago. They were in the place about fifty years and never wanted anything 'newfangled,'" Hal explained. "When I moved in I installed the pool but didn't bother to change anything else."

The truth was he rarely noticed his surroundings. He was always on the road with the team during the racing season or at the lab during the winter. The house had been just a place to get away from his grandfather.

But now Hal looked around critically. After all, this

was where Carlee was spending the majority of her time, and she was pregnant. He was pretty sure he'd heard somewhere that pregnant women should have pleasant surroundings, and she was right—the walls in here hadn't been painted for years. Whatever color they had originally been, it all looked kind of gray now, even after the cleaning.

"It sure needs painting," he agreed. "I'm never in here except to make a sandwich."

"But you do that so well."

"I'll get the decorators in. You buy whatever you want and don't worry about stepping on my toes. I can always throw it out again, can't I?"

She hesitated, her head on a tilt. "Would you—would you have time to come with me to look at a stove? I'd feel better if you approved."

So that afternoon found Hal wandering around the domestic appliances store at the mall with Carlee, examining stoves and listening to the salesman's somewhat inexpert pitch.

"Now, here's an eye-level gas oven and hob that's right at the top of the line," he said. "There's also an eye-level grill."

Carlee preferred cooking with gas. "Can you get gas installed, Hal?" she asked, obediently pulling open the oven to admire the number of jets and the easy-clean walls.

They solved that without trouble and were on their way to the cash desk to pay when Hal stopped in the refrigerator section.

"I guess we could use a new fridge, couldn't we?" he said. The salesman smiled. Carlee stopped and turned.

"A side-by-side would be nice," she agreed. The one Hal had now was an old-fashioned freezer-on-top kind, just like a yellow one her mother had had when Carlee was a toddler. Hal's was malfunctioning so severely she had to defrost it every few days.

"When would you like them delivered?" asked the salesman.

"Let's hold it. We'll get the decorators in first."

Carlee blew out a surprised breath. "Moving right along!"

"It's high time," he said, though the truth was he didn't understand what was driving him. If someone had whispered, "nesting instinct," he'd have run a mile, but no one did.

She had a field day at the next shop they visited, which sold cookware. Hal was astonished by the variety of pots and pans that she seemed to consider the basic minimum, but he was far from complaining. He was unexpectedly enjoying this shopping spree.

"Why don't you get this one?" he asked in front of the top-of-the-line model, when she chose a medium-priced food processor. "It's got more gadgets and stuff."

"It's certainly a superior model," chimed in the salesclerk, who was following them around.

"But it's twice the price, Hal," Carlee protested.

He looked at her in disbelief, but she was serious. "Carlee," he said gently. "Don't bother saving me a few bucks, okay? You get what you need."

"Hal! Hi!" said a voice, and he turned to see whose it was. Marietta Hunt was smiling at him, and belatedly the name of the shop registered. His friend

Tom had dated Marietta before his marriage a few years ago. She had three or four of these shops in her chain.

"Marietta, hi! Haven't seen you much lately," he said.

"I'm regularly at the club, Hal," she said. "Is this your wife? I heard you got married." She turned and smiled at Carlee. Since she'd never dated Hal and never particularly wanted to marry money, she had no bones to pick with his choice. "Marietta. Hi," she introduced herself.

"Carlee." Carlee smiled, and the two women shook hands.

"Carlee, this is Marietta Hunt," Hal said belatedly.

"I haven't seen *you* at the club, Carlee," Marietta observed.

"No, I haven't been."

"Well, if you wait for Hal to take you, you may wait all year. Shall I drop by tomorrow and pick you up? We've got a very nice pool and tennis courts. Do you play?"

Carlee's cheeks felt hot. "I do play, but not just at the moment," she said, glancing at Hal for help.

"Oh, that's too bad. Have you had an injury?"

"Yeah, I..." It was astonishing to Carlee now that they had never once considered what he would tell his friends, or whether she would join his social set.

"Carlee's pregnant," Hal interrupted.

"Really? That's wonderful! Congratulations!" said Marietta. Hal could see her telephone finger was already itching, and knew the die was cast. A smile pulled at his lips, which he thought was amusement with the gossip circuit, but which Marietta would later describe as, "Hal looks *so* proud!"

"Shall I pick you up tomorrow about one, and we'll go to the club for lunch?" Marietta suggested to Carlee, but Hal said, "Thanks, Marietta, I'll take Carlee myself tomorrow."

Marietta mocked him with wide eyes. "Goodness, how will the track stand your absence?" she said, which was unjust, because until the day Sharon and Maddie had snubbed him he'd been there most Sundays for an hour or so. But with fingers twinkling in farewell, Marietta left them before he could say so.

After that, Hal took a curious pleasure in buying Carlee a whole host of little gadgets that she clearly considered luxury items. "What do you do with that?" he asked as she paused before a shelf.

Carlee said, "It's an electric saucier."

"Would you like one?" he persisted.

"I've always made sauces over the stove."

"You're pregnant now. Standing over a hot stove will probably make you feel sick."

Carlee capitulated. "I'd love one. It would save so much time. When I go home I'll be so spoiled life just won't be the same."

He didn't particularly like her referring so casually to going home, as though she was determined that the intervening year would have no impact on her life, but she wasn't saying anything he could argue with. He'd have been a lot more annoyed if she hadn't said this at a moment when the salesclerk had gone to investigate something in the stock room for them, but no one was within earshot.

"You can take the saucier when you go," was all he said.

Outside again a few minutes later, Carlee paused in front of a brick-and-pine-decorated towel boutique.

"Do I need replacement towels, too?" Hal asked.

"Are you for real? You don't have towels, Hal, you have rags. But if you're serious about decorating, you should choose the bathroom colors before buying any."

Hal was getting the hang of this shopping thing and discovered he didn't want it to be over yet.

"I'm not much good at color schemes," he heard himself say. "Anyway, you'll notice it more than I will, being there all day. Let's say you choose."

Carlee looked away. This whole scenario was just too darn seductive. If she wasn't really careful she'd be asking Hal to admire knitted booties next. "I'll only be around a few months, Hal, there's no point in imposing my taste on you," she said in a low voice.

Possibly he had been spoiled by the women he was used to dating, a number of whom had regularly suggested that they had a talent in that direction and offered to supervise the redecoration of his house; a strong instinct for self-preservation had kept him from taking up any such offers. Now the tables were being turned, and he didn't like the feeling at all. He knew his irritation was irrational, but that only annoyed him more.

"The point is that your taste is probably going to be better than mine. I don't know much about color."

They were still standing at the boutique window, looking in, like expectant couples the world over.

Carlee turned her head as a sudden thought assailed her. "Are you color-blind?"

Hal blinked. "Curve ball," he observed dispassionately.

"It wasn't on the medical data sheet that Cyber-future sent me. Are you?"

"No, I'm not color-blind!" he said, offended, as he got her drift.

"There's no need to get in a snit."

"What would you do if I was? Dammit, stop treating me like a sperm donor!"

"Just, when you said your color sense wasn't good, I wondered, that's all," Carlee said pacifically.

"I'm asking you to help me decorate the place! I thought you'd enjoy it." He wouldn't have let Sharon within a mile of his bathroom color scheme, but here he was trying to *force* Carlee. "I thought women *liked* interior decoration."

Carlee remembered when she and Bryan had begun to decorate the house. Days so full of hope and planning. That had all been cut short the day he had fainted on a stepladder. She could feel the yearning in her for that kind of sharing—all the stronger, no doubt, because of pregnancy hormones. But it would do her no good to start anything like that with Hal.

"What if you didn't like it when it was done? You'll be living with it. If *I* don't like *your* choice, at least I'll only suffer for a year. The other way around, you might suffer for decades," she said, trying for humor.

"Could you keep your voice down?" When he thought of how he had given up all hope of a sex life for the duration, to protect Carlee from gossip, he was infuriated at how casually she was prepared to announce to whoever might be passing that the marriage had a preappointed end.

"I'm not shouting. Hal, what is your problem?"

His problem was he'd had years of women acting as if he was the catch of the decade, and for pretty much the first time in his life, a woman was determined to keep him at arm's length.

He just didn't like the feeling.

It was an education, taking Carlee to the club. She was so unlike the women who hung out there looking for their next husbands she was practically a different species. At first Hal couldn't figure out just what the difference was, because he'd seen nothing but the club type of woman, or track groupies, for so long he had never noticed their distinguishing characteristic.

But after a moment, he pinpointed it: Carlee didn't *pose;* she didn't sit in self-consciously unstudied postures that showed off her legs or breasts; she didn't make a show of half-jaded sophistication; and she didn't play as if unselfconsciously with her hair.

She had a natural animal femininity and grace, however, that meant that whatever her posture, she was somehow attractive to look at. And Hal was clearly not the only one who thought so.

Everyone who knew him was eager for an introduction, by which Hal guessed that his sudden marriage had been a hot topic on the gossip circuit. Carlee was surrounded by half a dozen people when Tom came up to claim Hal for their prelunch squash game.

Suddenly feeling protective, Hal wondered how

Carlee would cope if he went off leaving her in the lion's den.

"Carlee," he said, when he could get her attention. "Tom's here."

"Oh, hi, Tom!" she said cheerfully. She'd met Tom at the house but still hadn't visited his family. "How's everybody?"

"Just fine." Tom was grinning; he liked Carlee in that kind of direct, fundamental way that meant he felt happier in her presence. "Mind if I drag the groom off for a game of squash?"

She rolled her eyes. "Don't ask *my* permission!" she exclaimed, then turned to Hal. "Will I see you back here?"

"We've got the court booked for forty-five minutes. We'll go to lunch after that," he said, watching her for signs of anxiety or distress. She could always come and watch the game if being left on her own made her nervous. He wouldn't mind that, though he didn't normally like women watching his game.

"I'll probably have a swim, then," she said cheerfully. "So if I'm not here, will you check by the pool?"

He liked independent, self-sufficient women. There was no reason at all why this casual dismissal should irritate him. Nor could he understand why it did.

He was off his game. He felt hot, and kept thinking he'd rather be in the pool cooling off.

"I guess your injury's still affecting you," Tom excused him, and he didn't argue. When the game was over, he showered quickly and changed into his swim trunks and went out to the pool.

Carlee was on the diving board as he stepped out, bouncing lightly, preparatory to a dive. Her richly tropical multicolored bathing suit had flounces at the hips, emphasising her curvy shape in a way none of the svelte Cantabria beauties would have allowed even on their more slim-line shapes. Her skin was only a pale tan compared to many of the sun-hardened skins draped on the various loungers at the poolside, but she looked healthy and outdoorsy.

Her neat, compact little body arched up and then down, and cut the water with a seal's grace. She was halfway down the pool's length before she broke surface. She immediately turned to face back to the board and shouted something.

Hal looked up in time to see Jack Cooke, tanned, muscled, handsome, twice-married, and according to rumor, about to be divorced again, go off the board in a practiced dive. Seconds later he surfaced close beside Carlee, flashing a crinkly smile—and a medallion of some kind, which he held up and waved triumphantly.

"How did you *do* that?" Carlee wailed. "I dropped it as soon as I went in!"

"I know you did. Sneaky," he accused her.

"I thought you wouldn't see it for bubbles."

"Ah, but I found it by touch," said Jack seductively.

Carlee only laughed, but Hal found himself marching down the length of the pool toward the diving board, bouncing noisily and then executing an appallingly show-off jackknife dive—which Carlee did not notice—with ruthless precision. He saw Carlee and Jack swimming by over his head and surfaced beside her, catching her in his arms.

"Hi," he said.

"*Hal,* my goodness, you startled the life out of me!"

"Ready for lunch?"

"Hal, how's it going," said Jack Cooke, treading water beside them.

"Jack," he said, nodding dismissively, not looking away from Carlee's laughing face. His arms were around her, resting lightly against her waist and hips, and he felt the lustful impulse to sink under the surface, pull her tight against him and kiss her.

Hell, they all think we're newlyweds, he thought, and did it.

Her mouth was soft, full and firm, just like her body, and he could feel the heat rise in him in response and abruptly let her go.

"Hal, what are you doing?" she whispered in hoarse indignation when they surfaced again.

"Irresistible impulse."

"Well, cut it out!"

Just for the moment they were alone in the water. Jack had got the message and was preparing to dive again, and most other swimmers were drifting off to get ready for lunch.

"You don't want to mess with Jack," he murmured placatingly, afraid she'd belt him if he didn't have a good excuse. "And if I didn't react to him moving in on you, everybody in the club would know there was something wrong with our marriage."

"You didn't have to kiss me," she accused.

"That was just purely selfish," he agreed.

Carlee could feel the heat in her, and her heart quailed. She'd felt right at home in Hal's arms, and her mouth felt puffy, as if a whole bunch of cells had rushed to her lips to get a taste of his kiss and now were too drunk to go home. She suddenly realized, in addition to every other temptation, how easy it would be to fall for Hal physically.

She sure didn't need *that* kind of complication. It would be very, very dangerous. Carlee decided she'd better figure firmer ways to keep him at a distance if he ever showed signs of being purely selfish again.

10

In the end, Carlee could not resist the twin blandishments of an unlimited budget and a beautiful old house. She was seduced into excitement, planning and anticipation.

Hal had no idea that the mere act of sitting over paint chips and wallpaper books and design sketches with a partner could be so involving and so pleasant. He would be eternally grateful that he had never allowed someone like Sharon to get him into this, because as far as he could see, the process itself was dangerous. There was just something about it that seemed to promote bonding. Suppose, out of sheer inertia, he'd ended up letting Sharon move in? He had always known *that* would be a mistake.

He found living with Carlee easy, except that she was constantly running for cover. Like when, as they got around to discussing the third bedroom, Hal suddenly said, "You know, we really ought to turn it into the baby's room if we don't want my grandfather butting in with some scheme to have him up at the big house."

This brought Carlee back to earth with a bump. Playing house with Hal was dangerous in more ways than one. To create a room for her baby here would cause complications she could never deal with.

"We don't need a baby's room," she said flatly. "The baby and I will only be here for a few months after the birth, and we can share my room."

Hal could feel that she'd gone stiff, without being within miles of guessing why. "If we don't want The Two figuring that we've made a prior agreement and have him work to sabotage it, we should act normal," he said. "Normal people do up a baby's room."

"I don't believe in isolating a baby immediately after birth, anyway," she protested. "A newborn baby's never been alone all its life, and suddenly there it is in a giant lonely space...."

"We can knock a door through into your bedroom," countered Hal.

Carlee sighed for the bright little room at home in Buck Falls that she had planned to decorate for the baby. She looked at Hal. "Just so long as you don't start to imagine that the baby will be in that room on a permanent basis." But of course it was herself she was warning.

"Dammit, woman!" Hal exploded as the reasons for her resistance abruptly seemed plain. "Could you stop being so paranoid? I gave you my word!"

And Carlee could not resist the temptation to make a special room for her baby, even though she knew it would make her hope for something she didn't want to name.

That week Hal joined the Chelven Light team in Japan for the Grand Prix. His doctors warned him it was too soon, that the torn muscles and broken bones hadn't yet recovered, but Hal was used to hearing things like that, and the doctors were used to their advice being ignored, so everyone was happy.

Except Carlee. She said goodbye to him with a cheerful smile and wished him luck, while her heart thudded with a hideous dread like nothing she had ever felt before. She could feel something beating in her, slow and horrible, that was not her heart, and her imagination said it was a death knell.

She had wanted to beg him not to go, had wished she could tell him about this awful feeling of doom. But she herself had no rights over him, and if she had said, *for the sake of the baby, please don't go,* what did that mean to a man who loved nothing so much as freedom? So she had said nothing.

She had not even been able to say, "Phone me when you get there," so she spent a wakeful night cruising the cable news channels, waiting to be told of disaster.

His plane arrived safely, but the heavy feeling didn't stop, and it was then that Carlee started to pray, because she knew it was the race that was the danger.

She knew that if it happened she could not bear to hear it from someone else, could not bear not to know the moment it happened. She knew she had to sit in front of the television and watch.

She didn't think of having company, so obsessed was she with the event and her fears. But when she heard the doorbell five minutes before race time, and Marietta Hunt stood on the step, smiling and saying, "You can't possibly watch this race by yourself," Carlee almost fell on her neck with gratitude.

"I'll get the drinks and snacks," Marietta said masterfully. "You go and watch, or you'll be a basket case."

He was not driving a winning race, that was clear, or not at the start. He was pacing himself, giving himself time to get back into it, and Carlee began insensibly to relax. Of course he wouldn't push it; she should have realized that. Not with his injuries still so fresh, his reactions bound to be affected.

It happened on the seventeenth lap, like lightning from a clear sky. A sound like a bullet, and then Vassily Vathek, who had been trading places with Hal for the last two laps, went out of control.

"Vathek's lost a tire!" shouted the commentator.

"No!" screamed Marietta, because Vathek was heading at an angle across the track, and the car immediately behind him was the Chelven Light car of Hal Ward.

Carlee did not cry out. Her whole being was concentrated in a pinpoint of light as she stared at the screen, and it seemed to her that she shot that light of her being heavenward, pleading for his life with all that she was.

Vassily Vathek's car hit the retaining wall just in front of Hal and bounced back. And as if he had known the exact trajectory in advance, Hal steered a straight course between Vathek and the wall, with inches to spare.

The two women clutched each other and burst into tears.

Hal finished a humiliating third from last and knew it was too soon after the injury. Pain affected his concentration, and when his concentration was broken he was thinking about Carlee. That had never happened to him before. He began to take a long hard look at himself.

Hal was right about The Two. He hadn't given up, he was merely holding a watching brief. On the morning the decorators and carpenters and plumbers descended, TT's housekeeper arrived with an invitation to Carlee to lunch with the old man.

Carlee thanked her and said no, and the next person she saw coming through the kitchen door was The Two himself.

"You can't sleep here surrounded by all these toxic fumes!" he said angrily, before they'd even exchanged greetings. "It might harm the baby. You'll have to come and stay at the house until the work is finished. I've had the housekeeper prepare your old room."

Carlee looked at the old man steadily for a long moment of silence. "You know," she said at last, "I'm amazed that a man with so much business success has so little understanding of human nature. Is this how you've been dealing with Hal all these years? No wonder you made such a mess of it."

"Pardon?" The Two's head of steam died under this confusing sideswipe.

"You come storming in here telling me what to do when it's absolutely none of your business—what do you expect out of this kind of approach?"

"What?"

He was actually speechless. Carlee, who was finding it very hard at the moment to forget the accident and what it would have meant, and was blaming it all on The Two, took the opportunity to get things off her chest.

"Nobody of any intelligence who'd tried that approach once could ever imagine it was going to work on any normal person, but I hear you've been using it on Hal as a regular thing, and now here you are trying it on me! You already know me well enough to understand that it won't work on me any more than it does on Hal. So maybe you ought to ask yourself what you really want when you act in such a stupid way. I mean, Harlan, do you really want to protect my baby from potentially toxic fumes, or do you just want a fight?"

His eyes fixed on her throughout this barrage of words, Harlan de Vouvray Ward II groped for a chair and sank into it. "I want to protect your baby," he said, but the usual note of authority was gone from his voice.

"Well, good," said Carlee with an approving nod, in the same tone she would have used with one of her less bright grade sixes. "And what do you think I want? Do you think I want my baby to be healthy, or do you think I'm determined to make it brain damaged if I possibly can?"

"That's a ridiculous question!" he stormed.

"It's ridiculous to think I would ever hurt my baby, but it's not ridiculous to ask if that's what's in your mind, because that's what comes across from your attitude. And naturally I resent it. Like Hal, I also hate being told what to do, and if it were anything less important than my baby's health, I can see where you'd drive a person right into opposition, whatever my previous intentions had been.''

Harlan de Vouvray Ward II never apologized. "That's not what I meant," he said gruffly.

"Maybe another time you could ask me first what my plans are, instead of assuming I'm a brainless fool and trying to lay down the law to me. And you might also remind yourself that I am an adult of sound mind and full civil rights. Now, thank you for your concern, Harlan, but it is unnecessary, and if you'll excuse me, I have work to do.''

He stood up, a beaten man. "What *are* your plans?"

She looked at him.

"If you don't mind my asking," he managed to get out.

"I've booked into a hotel for the duration."

"If you'd prefer to stay with me, your room is ready whenever you want," he said feebly.

"Thank you, that might suit me better. Would you mind if I let you know later on?"

It was while she was sleeping at the big house during the period of the redecoration that Carlee awoke to feel the baby move in her for the first time. Just the tiniest flutter in her abdomen, but suddenly the world was a changed place.

She laid a hand protectively over her womb and wished there were someone to tell about this deep magic. If Hal were home, she knew she would have gone to wake him, to share this unbelievably significant moment with him, and the knowledge that on a deep, primitive level she wished she could was one more proof that her feelings might be getting out of control.

She would have to be much more careful now. She must not allow herself to get emotionally involved with him; it would only break her heart in the end.

The doctor ordered Hal off the team and home, something he didn't mind at all. At the moment he was far more interested in progress at the lab than on the track; he couldn't really understand what had driven him to go to Japan in the first place.

"Hi," he said softly, coming into the kitchen late one afternoon to find Carlee writing a recipe at the new oak table they had chosen.

"Hal!" She had not been expecting him for another hour. Carlee dropped her pen and jumped up so suddenly that her chair fell over. "You're home!"

He was surprised at how relieved he was to be seeing Carlee again. He'd had close shaves before, but never before had he looked at a woman and been so fervently glad he was still alive.

So before they knew it, there they were, wrapped in each other's arms, hugging hard. And then Hal bent and did what he'd been wanting to do again ever since that day in the pool.

Carlee almost fainted with the strength of sheer physical feeling that coursed up and down her body from head to toes at the touch of his mouth. She clung to him, slipping her arms up around his neck so that their bodies were pressed together, and opened her mouth hungrily under his.

Hal lost it. The man who'd always prided himself on staying cool developed an instant fused brain. He wrapped his arms tightly around her and took full advantage of her parted lips. The sweet tang of her was something he would never get enough of; that was about all he knew. But he stood there trying, pressing and licking and sucking her lips and stuffing his pollen sacs till they almost burst.

Some part of his brain still had basic functional capacity, he could still walk; he found he was leading her up the stairs, which he belatedly figured was a good idea. There was a doorknob under his hand, and he could still turn that.

Carlee felt a pressure under her back and knew she was on the bed, but it was the pressure on top of her that took all her concentration. Hal's body felt so right, so right, and she wrapped her arms around him and tried to draw him closer than gravity did. She felt enveloped by his arms, his legs, his desire, and that was what she wanted.

He held her head and kissed her mouth till they were both drunk on sensation. "Carlee," he whispered urgently. "Carlee." There was pleading in his tone. He had never begged any woman for anything, but he wasn't thinking of that now. It was because it wasn't sex alone he needed, it was something else. It was as though he was asking for her essential self. Something he'd never needed from anyone before.

She was wearing a loose cotton dress that buttoned down the front, and when he opened that, her full, rich breasts were revealed to him with a suddenness that took his breath away. He bent to kiss and suck them while she stroked his hair and pressed him closer.

She pulled his shirt out of his waistband so that she

could feel the heat of his back, and he raised himself on an elbow and dragged it over his head, and then his chest was hot against her breasts and she moaned with the joy of it.

When he entered her they both cried out wildly, in the amazement of the discovery of a new country. He thrust into her with long, slow strokes that drove her crazy with anticipation, and watched how her face contorted with her concentration on pleasure.

"Oh, Hal, that feels wonderful!" she whispered, mewing as each stroke reached home.

"Carlee, you're so beautiful and you feel so good," he said, wishing he had the words to say what he really meant. They were there, just hovering at the edge of his mental vision, but he couldn't catch them.

His hand caught her hip, her thigh, and pressed so that she felt he would never let her go, and she began to tremble as tears burned her eyes. "Hold me, hold me!" she begged, and he did, as the surprise of pleasure rushed through her whole being, body and soul.

She sobbed, and he could not contain his response. The long slow stroking gave way to firm thrusts as he cried her name in his search for pleasure, and as he found it, it fountained up again in her, so deep within her being she seemed attached to the stars.

They cried each other's name once, and in answer heard the perfect stillness of eternity.

She had done something irrevocable, had visited a place in herself she should never have gone. The place where she had been hiding her love for him.

Dangerous, dangerous mistake.

* * *

Later they swam, and later still, they ate a meal. They did not talk about what had happened between them. She knew that he would not say what she hoped to hear, that the best she could do now was pretend to herself it hadn't happened and make sure it never happened again.

"But I just realized you haven't seen the place yet!" she exclaimed brightly, when they had eaten and Hal started smiling at her in a way that was going to pull her apart if she didn't stop him.

"I wasn't really looking," he agreed with a slow grin.

"Come and look!" she commanded, grabbing his hand and turning away to hide the heat in her cheeks. "It's all finished, it's just beautiful."

There was a sense of sharing as they walked around viewing the results of their collaboration, which no longer astonished Hal. He felt nothing would surprise him about his feelings for Carlee anymore.

It was her dream house. The kitchen, in two shades of Wedgwood blue, had pale oak cupboards and a terra-cotta tile floor, with a freestanding butcher's block workspace. Shelves holding her cookbooks and tall jars filled with things like lentils and spaghetti, and decorated with green trailing plants, lined the walls. A square oak table and chairs had replaced the chrome and arborite model against the wall where the stove and fridge had once been; a massive Dutch cupboard filled with blue and cream crockery dominated one corner.

"Now, this is a real working kitchen," Hal said approvingly.

"Yeah," Carlee agreed softly. "The best I've ever

worked in. Thanks, Hal.'' It was a kitchen to cook in, to live in, to make the centre of a home.

The living room, with a new blond oak floor and cream-colored walls and area rugs and sofas uphol- stered with brightly woven kilims, was now filled with light, where before it had seemed gloomy. The dining room, newly furnished in elm, its cabinets filled with expensive new china and crystal, had wide new doors opening out to a small, tree-shaded side terrace, festooned with plants, and furnished in natural wicker and thickly stuffed canvas cushions in navy with white piping.

"It's just perfect for entertaining, don't you think?" Carlee babbled excitedly. "It came out just the way we imagined."

She didn't notice that she was hanging confidingly on his arm, but Hal did. He looked down at her. Her long hair, just washed, was floating loose around her shoulders and looked as soft as a kitten's fur. He lifted a hand to stroke it, but she bent forward to pluck a dead leaf from a plant.

Only the baby's room remained to be furnished. They had decorated it in soft green and white with one wall of baby wallpaper, but the furniture was still an adult double bed and dresser. Hal sometimes brought one or other of his designers or engineers home for dinner, and afterward they would work till late in his study. So they had left the baby's room as a guest room for the time being. Carlee had moved into the master bedroom, where Hal used to sleep, and a door connected it to the baby's room. Hal opened the door and looked through to where the bed was a confusion of sheets and pillows and the memory of their lovemaking. He smiled at her, but Carlee turned away.

"I don't know what we're going to do for a guest room when the baby comes!" she babbled. Hal said nothing, but somehow the answer to that was so obvious it seemed to hit her in the face. Carlee bit her lip. "Well, it won't be for very long, anyway," she reminded them both, and for both of them, standing there in their baby's room, the words rang awkwardly false.

There was excitement at the lab. As so often happens when a group of people have been working with persistence and dedication for years, success came "overnight" to the lab team. On his first morning back, Hal walked in to face a phalanx of grinning team members.

"Man, are we glad you didn't bite the dust in Japan, Hal!" Trevor exclaimed jovially.

Hal didn't usually get a welcoming committee when he got back from the road, so he looked closely at them. Most of the team, he noticed, looked as if they had died three days ago and were still staggering around. Most hadn't shaved since he'd gone, and they all looked as though they'd been taking in nothing but coffee. They stank, too.

"What the hell?" Hal said conversationally. "You guys been held hostage by the Seven Sisters since I've been gone, or have you just taken to producing armpit Gorgonzola?"

He knew, of course, and they knew he knew.

"It's a nice little earner, armpit Gorgonzola," said Barry. "You'd be surprised."

"That's a relief. So you've got an alternate career if we close this project down."

Trev, grinning, scratched his hairy chin. "Yeah, but probably you won't want to do that yet awhile, Hal."

Suddenly they were whooping and laughing and clapping Hal and each other on the back. "This is it, Hal!" "We've done it!" they cried, and took him to show him their results.

It wasn't by any means the first such breakthrough the team had experienced together—what made it special was that it was the *last*. Now they knew exactly where they were going, and how to get there. Now it was just work.

One seductively intimate area of communication that Carlee could not avoid was the baby. As the child in her made its presence more and more felt, she found she simply could not resist the temptation to plan and dream about its future with Hal. And Hal was always willing to engage in such dreaming.

"If he takes after the Wards, there's no point hoping he'll be anything sane like an accountant," Hal warned her once. "More likely to be a pirate."

"I'd like to see any child of mine growing up on the wrong side of the law," Carlee said, with a militant light in her eye.

Hal grinned. Her hair always ruffled when she was moved, and he found her indignation engaging. Sometimes he couldn't resist the temptation to ignite it. "How are you going to stop him?"

She gazed at him in wide-eyed disbelief. "I am going to teach him—or her—the difference between right and wrong, that's how!'' she said. "Myself! I'm not going to leave it to television or worse."

"And what is right, and what is wrong?" he asked gently.

"You need me to tell you that?" she asked ironically.

Hal grinned in acknowledgment of her check. He'd been hoping to sucker her into a lecture. "Not everybody who knows the difference between right and wrong chooses the right, do they?" he tried again.

"If you teach them right, and nothing really bad happens to them, of course they do."

"Do you teach your grade sixes right and wrong?"

"Naturally. Some of them grow up with the television as a baby-sitter. If I don't teach them, no one will."

"Tell me what you teach them," he asked softly, meaning it, and suddenly they were involved in a discussion of truth and goodness and love.

These conversations with Carlee had a curious impact on Hal. The thing was, no one had dreamed of talking to Hal like this since those deep, long ago philosophical discussions at high school parties. Hal was known to be reckless, wild, a rebel, a playboy, who cared for nothing. Any woman who did have deeper thoughts than this season's choice of hair color would certainly never have let on to Hal. Every woman he knew was devoted to fun, or pretended to be. Morals and religion were not chic at the Cantabria County Country Club.

He liked the fact that Carlee didn't care about his opinion or anyone else's when it came to such matters. One day at the club, listening to the recital of one of Jack Cooke's more unpleasant exploits, Carlee had brought total silence on a laughing, jokey group by asking, "But Jack, don't you think what you did was wrong?"

Jack recovered quickly from the unexpected blow. "Wrong from whose point of view?" he asked with a sardonic smile.

"From the point of view of right and wrong. What you did must have hurt her feelings, when I bet she thought you liked her."

And just like that, with all the éclat of a central truth, everybody suddenly understood that Jack Cooke's central motivation was hatred of women.

Carlee was by no means universally popular at the Cantabria County Country Club.

She was popular with the people closest to him, though. They saw Gerry and Sheila Maitland regularly after the night they'd come to dinner, bringing the new baby. And the members of Hal's research team were always finding excuses for working with Hal at the house, and it wasn't entirely because they wanted to eat Carlee's cooking. They also liked talking to her.

Tom and Gemma and their daughter Ellie were also regular visitors at the house, whether Hal was home from the lab or not. Carlee had made friends with Marietta Hunt, too. She tended to like, and be liked by, people who actually worked for a living, whether they had to or not. It was the loungers and scroungers who were uncomfortable around Carlee.

Hal came home dusty but jubilant from a test drive that had not been without complications, but was nevertheless conclusive. The first thought on his mind all morning had been to tell Carlee the news.

He found Gerry Maitland by the pool, deep in intimate conversation with a fascinated Carlee, who was hanging on his words. Neither of them noticed Hal's approach, though he didn't consciously sneak up on them.

"Night's falling over the lake now. A half moon. The campfire is burning low. The two sisters are sitting on rocks, silhouetted against the glittering water. Their voices murmuring. Lena's leaning against the big pine tree, listening to them without taking it in. Suddenly one sentence comes out of the murmur..."

With a rueful smile, Hal realized that Gerry was trying out his film plot on her. *Take a number, Hal,* he told himself irritably, damned if he'd line up to whisper his achievements in his own wife's ear. Just then they became aware of his presence and looked up blinking.

"Hal!" exclaimed Gerry, jumping up.

"Hi, you're home for lunch?" said Carlee with a wide smile. She seemed distracted, as if she were still absorbed in Ger's plot.

Waving a hand, Hal sank onto a nearby lounger. "Don't let me interrupt, Ger, the story sounds great."

But Gerry shook his head. "No, no, it's not ready for the public yet."

Hal found it more than a little galling that *he,* who had known Gerry for nearly fourteen years, was "the public," while Carlee, apparently, was not.

"It just sounds *great,* so far, Gerry," Carlee enthused. "Let's have lunch now, and you can tell me the rest when Hal's gone back to the lab."

Since Hal had never been jealous of anyone in his life before, he had no idea what the feeling was that made him want to throw Ger in the pool all of a sudden.

All he knew was he didn't like it.

11

When he thought of it afterward, he was glad Gerry had been there. There were difficulties around telling Carlee about their success at the lab, difficulties he maybe hadn't given sufficient weight to in that first heady excitement of success. Like—before he could tell her about the breakthrough, he had to admit he'd been lying to her and everyone about the work they were doing.

Of course, Carlee would understand the need for secrecy, and once he got going he'd be fine, but he just couldn't figure out how to begin.

Second, he'd promised her she could go home as soon as the research had got to a certain stage, and she was bound to ask if they were at that stage, and it would be impossible to lie about it. She would want to go home, but how could he let her go home now, when her house in Buck Falls was rented for a whole year, and they were booked to start Lamaze classes soon?

And third, and not least of the difficulties, was the fact that Carlee was being really elusive these days. She seemed to shy off any conversation not about the weather.

So Hal would build up a head of steam, get the intro all worked out in his head...

"Good day at the lab?" Carlee asked, as she did every day. It was a ritual kind of question, offhand. The question of a woman who doesn't want an in-depth answer.

"Really good," said Hal. "A terrific day. Trev and..."

"That's nice. What do you want to drink? I got some imported Czech beer at Monique's today, do you want to try it?"

It drove him crazy. The more he tried to get close, the more she shut down.

He remembered times—many times—when things had been the other way around. When it was a woman who accused him of "avoiding intimacy." He hadn't really understood what they'd meant. Suddenly, now, he did.

Avoiding intimacy was when, watching a film with her, he moved to put an arm around her shoulders and Carlee sat forward, so that he had to withdraw. *Avoiding intimacy* was when, at a club, he drew her close for a slow dance, and after a moment of what seemed to him like real shared pleasure, Carlee went stiff and said, "Hal."

"Mmm?" asked Hal dreamily. Her belly was start-ing to show, and he could feel the swelling against his abdomen.

"Is there someone here you're trying to convince this is a real marriage for some reason?"

Once, stroking her braid as they sat by the pool at sunset, he'd whispered, "Rapunzel, Rapunzel, let down thy hair," and she had gently but unmistakably pulled her hair from his hold and started to talk about something.

Avoiding intimacy had a hundred forms. All of them irritated and confused him, because they threw him off balance. Hal wasn't sure himself what he wanted. But he knew he had to know before he could force the issue with Carlee. It wouldn't be fair to her to shatter her self-sufficiency and then discover that wasn't what he wanted. But how was he going to find out when she kept him at arm's length?

No other woman had ever raised that instinct in him to protect her from himself. He'd never been so challenged, never tried to examine his feelings for a woman so minutely before.

Also, suppose he got sure about what he wanted, and then found out that Carlee just didn't find him attractive and never would? He'd never before really been afraid of something like that, but he was now. They hadn't talked anything over after they'd made love. He got the idea that Carlee was trying to pretend it just hadn't happened. He'd thought she enjoyed their lovemaking as much as he did, but he was uneasily aware that he could be wrong. She'd cried. At the time he'd thought it was because she was so deeply touched. But maybe he was wrong. Maybe she'd felt she was betraying Bryan. Or maybe he just didn't turn Carlee on.

The whole thing was destabilizing him.

Carlee was having a bad time. She understood so much now, when it was too late. One of the biggest mistakes she'd made was to imagine, after Bryan's death, that she would not fall in love again. That conviction had made her feel immune to any danger from Hal till it was too late.

Another bad mistake was her assumption that, having loved once, she would recognize love if it *did* ever come her way again. But what she felt for Hal was so different from what she had felt for Bryan that it had been ages before she began to see how dangerous it was.

She had known and loved Bryan virtually all her life. It had been a love founded and rooted in their long history, in shared moments, a shared life. Bryan and she had grown up together, had faced new experiences together, had made love for the first time with each other, and never with anyone else... learning and sharing together had made them part of each other.

With Hal it was very different. Her relationship with Hal was full of sparkle and excitement, as well as the deep, primitively physical understanding that he was the father of the child inside her. It was a much more fundamental, basic, almost cellular attraction she felt for him.

This made it deeply dangerous, because her feelings were not comfortable and serene but volatile and unpredictable. Sometimes, sitting at the dining table, watching Hal put the food she had cooked into his mouth, she would feel the blood suddenly begin to race around her system in crazy sexual excitement. Or simply catching his eye unexpectedly, she was moved by a feeling so overwhelming she couldn't breathe. When she saw him unexpectedly, like that day he came for lunch when she was with Gerry Maitland by the pool, she had to practically grit her teeth not to climb all over him.

She knew he was happy with what was going on at the lab, suspected that they'd had a significant success. But she did not want to hear about it. How could she be glad about an engine that he would use to try and win the Grand Prix championship, when every race would make her sick with fear? And yet how could she not be glad that he had got the success he so wanted?

And the thought of his success also brought home to her the fact that this arrangement was temporary, that the sooner she let him tell her about his success, the sooner she would be going home.

She should let him tell her, but she couldn't. *Not yet,* she pleaded with the gods. *Just a little longer.*

She knew she was being a fool, putting off a moment that was already going to be as painful as she could take. She told herself that as long as she didn't allow any more intimacy, as long as she maintained her distance, she wasn't actually increasing her danger or her future hurt, just...delaying. That was all she was doing.

Dangerous, comfortable lies.

Once, as they sat by the pool watching a perfect sunset, chatting quietly about the baby and its possible future choices, the baby moved in her, telegraphing a deep contentment that was impossible to describe. It was as though—as though the baby felt not amniotic fluid but *love* surrounding itself, and stretched out within that love in a feeling of total trust.

She was very sure, on that intuitive level, that the

baby felt not just her own love for it, but Hal's as well. Whatever Hal thought, he was growing close to the baby.

She became increasingly torn. If he loved the baby, how would he ever be able to give it up? And if he could not give it up, what would happen to them all?

Carlee became jumpy, unsure of everything. She was unpredictable. Laughing with him one minute, withdrawing or shouting at him the next. One step forward, two steps back.

It didn't help, either, that pregnancy made her about the sexiest thing walking. No wonder he'd been able to resist intimacy with women like Sharon and Maddie, he realized. Thin women just didn't *move* him in the way that Carlee's luscious curves did, but he'd never realized that before. He'd always figured he got pretty turned on by those long, slender, manicured, bikini-waxed shapes.

Carlee was different. He was discovering, for example, that Carlee had two levels of natural body odors. The first was the ordinary level that everyone had—the smell of her skin, her sweat…he liked that level of odor in her, which he hadn't in all his women friends.

The other level was different. He couldn't name it, he couldn't even really smell it, he just knew it was there. If they danced, for example, and he breathed in that subliminal smell, he felt so physically and emotionally moved by her he felt he wanted to pull her right into his body, he wanted to crush her against him.

Fat lot of good it did him.

"What is it—they passed some kind of law in California while I wasn't looking?" he demanded irritably one night, when he had tried to get close and she'd slipped away yet again.

Carlee frowned. "Pardon?"

"There's a statutory six-inch space that has to be kept between a man and his wife, or what?"

She looked at him, long and level. "That's right," she said.

The really weird part was no other woman turned him on now. Even if they'd been willing, and there were those who'd indicated they might have had a change of heart, Hal was irritably aware that he'd now reached a point where only Carlee would do.

Fat, *fat* lot of good it did him.

At the end of September the Chelven Light team won the Grand Prix and returned home to an exuberant welcome on the day before Hal's birthday. No one had expected to win without Hal in the race, but John Hoight, the team's second-string driver, had come up with the right stuff when the two favorites had knocked each other out of the race in an accident with miraculously no injuries.

After a day of wild celebration in Cantabria, the team and their spouses and girlfriends naturally ended up at Hal's place for an impromptu party that lasted well into the night. Carlee found meeting these friends kind of thrilling. She'd never before come across the combination of the strong team bonding and leading-edge individualism of men who put their lives constantly at risk for the sake of personal glory.

There were so many people, and they all talked so

fast, that except for John Hoight, she found it impossible to sort out who was who or what job they performed with the team. So she wasn't really sure who exactly were the people a slightly drunk Hal casually invited to crash for the night rather than driving home. But a quick count assured her of one thing: with one man on each sofa, and one couple in the spare bedroom, there was nowhere for the second couple to whom Hal had generously extended his invitation to sleep.

"Hal," she protested softly, "Louise and Gilles are already taking the spare room."

"Ah, we'll find room," Hal said expansively. "Lots of space."

What followed was inevitable. Hal gave up his room to the second couple, and suddenly Hal and Carlee were going to have to share a bedroom. And a bed.

She did not need this. Carlee was practically at breaking point already with Hal. This might be more than she could take.

"What did you think you were playing at?" she hissed, when the house was silent at last, all the guests were bedded down and she was facing Hal across the width of her bed.

"You don't have to act as though I did it deliberately," Hal said indignantly, and suddenly all the pent-up feelings, all the emotional confusion and instability that both of them were feeling, exploded in an argument that lost none of its intensity through the fact that it was conducted at low volume. "I've had a lot of champagne. I forgot!"

"Forgot! Seven people you invite, and you *forget* there won't be room for them?"

"I'm used to having two spare rooms! Gilles and Ben and their wives always stay, they live in L.A. I just didn't think!"

"I don't believe anybody could be so stupid even drunk!"

"What's the big deal? You're spending the night with your lawful wedded husband and the father of your child, is that a problem?"

Carlee stared at him. It terrified her when he talked like that. Or half terrified, half disarmed her. But the very fact that it half disarmed her terrified her, so there she was back at full terror.

"What are you saying, Hal?" she demanded.

"Nothing that's not the truth! You're my wife! That's supposed to mean something, isn't it?"

"What is it supposed to mean? Is it supposed to mean you get free sex for the duration? I'm your wife in name only, remember? That was the deal. Nothing in the deal says you can come into my bedroom whenever you feel like it!"

"You didn't mind me coming into your bedroom when you had pregnancy sickness!"

"What the hell has that got to do with anything?"

"Why can't we change our minds about the deal?" he demanded, trying a new tack.

"How far do you want to change your mind? Just enough to get sex when you want it?"

"I don't see why we can't take one day at a time," he objected. "You never let me get close to you."

With a sudden jolt, hearing his own words, Hal

realized this was just the kind of accusation that he'd been on the *receiving* end of for years.

"You've never said you wanted to get close," she pointed out ruthlessly.

"Does everything have to be *words?*" he demanded helplessly. "You don't let me touch you. Why can't I touch you?"

She did not relent. "Why do you want to touch me?"

"Dammit, do we have to know everything in advance? How are we supposed to find out where we are if we don't let anything move?"

Abruptly Carlee cracked and began saying things she hardly even realized she felt. "I've already lost one man I loved!" she shouted hoarsely. "I'm not going to let myself love you, Hal, and then end up alone and empty again when you decide you've had enough. We have an agreement, and I intend to stick to it. I'm not going to try and turn my feelings on and off like a tap just so you don't feel left out or horny or whatever your problem is! You have no right to make demands of me when you know damned well you have nothing but sex on your mind! I'm pregnant, and that makes me emotionally vulnerable, and if you don't know that already, you'd better learn it right now, because I do not intend to put up with scenes like this for the next five months! What we did was a mistake, and I'm not going to make it again!"

"Who says I've got nothing but sex on my mind?" he demanded mulishly, blinking against the barrage of words.

"Well, what's on your mind, then—for the third, or is it the fourth time? What exactly do you want?"

He stood looking at her, full of confusion and desire, and fear and hope and love, unable to put any of it into words.

"What do *you* want?" he countered.

"I want stability and a loving home for my baby," she temporized. "Basic minimum. And that's not on offer, is it?"

"Why do you say that? Stability? I've got more to offer than most men, haven't I?"

She looked at him pityingly. "What, for example?"

"You'll never want for anything the rest of your life."

"Money's a very nice thing, but a woman needs more than money in a husband, and a child needs more in a father. I've got a baby to think of, Hal!" she said, and then, just as if the baby thought she should be thinking of it right now, she got a hard little kick right under her heart.

"Ow!" she cried, and her hand involuntarily went to her stomach, not that it hurt physically. But there was no doubt the baby didn't like the emotions she was feeling and wanted her to stop.

Every vestige of emotion drained from Hal's face. She had never seen anyone go so white. He was at her side in a microsecond. "What is it?" he said hoarsely. "Carlee, what's wrong?" Almost without knowing what he was doing, he put his hand on her belly.

She grabbed his hand, moved it to the site of activity, and pressed hard. "Would you like to feel what the baby thinks of this argument?" she asked.

He felt it then, a strange little ripple against his

palm, that was comparable to nothing else he had ever experienced on God's earth. "What is it?" he gasped breathlessly. "Is that him? What's he doing?"

"Just telling me to stop producing unpleasant hormones," Carlee said with a soft, sweet smile.

"My God, that's—is that my son?" Hal had never been so shaken. No feeling he'd ever felt in all his life came close to what he was feeling now.

"Or daughter."

She was surprised, and more than a little fearful, when Hal bent down and pressed his lips to the swell of her abdomen where the baby had been moving a moment ago.

"Okay, baby," he said. "Son or daughter. You're the boss. No more arguing. We're going to bed."

They did, too, with a lot less awkwardness than Carlee had imagined she would feel. She changed in the bathroom and got into bed, and when Hal emerged from the bathroom in a pair of cotton boxer shorts and crawled into bed beside her, it really didn't seem strange after all. It seemed natural.

She flicked off the bedside lamp, and they lay in darkness and silence for a few seconds, getting their bearings. Then Hal moved close, and it seemed natural to her to go into his arms.

"I'd like to make love to you, Carlee," he said. "But you were right in what you said. We can't just treat this as a casual affair. I'm going to think hard before I do anything that might hurt you."

Snuggled against his chest, she felt safe, as if all her fears were foolish. "All right," she said.

She fell asleep very quickly in his hold. When he

was sure she was asleep, Hal bent and kissed her forehead.

He had no idea what time it was when he awoke, nor what woke him. He lay on his side, curled into her back, her hips nestling into his groin, his arm protectively across her.

Under his hand, in a message just for him, the baby moved. Hal convulsively pressed his hand against Carlee's stomach, to be sure of what he'd felt, and, as if in response, the baby did it again.

Hello. That was what he heard, what he felt. He was sure he felt the baby's deep unconsciousness, like a dream state, and that in that dream the baby was aware of Hal as another consciousness, another self.

Then there was just the night, and Hal, and this tiny creature who was slowly entering the world through the strange door that was Carlee's body.

Suddenly Hal was thinking about his last near-accident. He had avoided it, and even as he did he had known it might have been fatal. He had been more than lucky to escape.

If he had died then, this child, like Hal himself, would have been born posthumously, with no chance of ever knowing his father. But the baby's position would have been far worse than that. With Hal dead, The Two would have pursued Carlee ruthlessly to get custody of the baby. She was a fighter, she had strength, it would have been a battle of the titans— but that battle, Hal knew, Carlee would have lost. In such a battle money would have had the final word.

Then history would have repeated itself, with The Two wrapping the baby in the same stifling overprotectiveness that Hal had so hated. And Carlee would have been worn down exactly as his own mother had been, fighting a hopeless battle to raise the child herself and finally giving up...becoming a lifeless shadow whose maternal caring had been turned against her.

All of this might still happen. He thought of the race he had run so recently, before his body was really ready. That moment of sudden pain that had broken his concentration—that was the kind of moment, at high speeds, that caused accidents.

Hal had never actually felt mortal before. His grandfather had yammered away at him without him ever feeling the threat of death as real. Danger...he felt that, and until a couple of years ago he had loved the edge it put on life. Now he was older, and his pleasure was more in the skill, the science of the race, than in the danger.

He understood suddenly, for the first time, that he could find that same pleasure in many other things. The thrill of danger could only be found in life-threatening activity. These other pleasures he was finding every day in the lab.

Carlee was right when she had said, more or less, that Hal had nothing to offer a woman. His money would have satisfied most of the women he knew, but what did he have to offer Carlee—a woman worth a man's best? He wasn't even a man, he saw. He hadn't had the guts to stand up to the old man for her sake, for the sake of her well-being and their child's. He had abandoned her to his grandfather's power.

He realized then, for the first time, that if he had ever really stood up to the old man, he would have won. If he had said, "Leave her alone," and had been willing to take the risk like a man—The Two would have had to back down. He had *allowed* the old man to run him.

Carlee had been right about his rebellion. His life had been spent, not in forging his own path, as he had always imagined, but in reacting against the old man's dictates and wishes.

What legacy would he leave this child if he died in his next race? A half-finished experiment in the lab that would almost certainly die from lack of funding and legal red tape. The image of a father who was a throwback to the family pirate, who had made no useful contribution to anything, not even to his own child's upbringing. A father with a reputation as a playboy, who had not had enough commitment to produce a child through normal loving or even through passionate error, but only through a mistake in an insemination procedure.

He thought of his work, the new engine. This at least had come from his inner self, the man he truly was. *That* was where his future lay. He felt it in his bones, the engineers felt it. If they were right, he and his team would have a share of the glory of those who, through the ages, have made contributions to the world. That was a legacy worth leaving a child. That was a man's work. That was something to live up to.

Under his hand, the baby was active, a nocturnal creature whispering and rustling in the darkness, pushing against his hand now and then as though for reassurance.

Carlee murmured and stirred in her sleep, brushing against his loins, and he was suddenly suffused with powerful desire for them both, his wife and his child, a desire at once mental, physical and spiritual. He wanted to make love to Carlee, he wanted to hold and know the child that was part of them both, he wanted to feel that they were all a part of each other...

Sometimes the darkness of night brings a clarity the day can never offer. Hal could see, as if it were painted for him on the canvas of his mind, two roads diverging in a wood. He stood at the fork.

Dammit, he said to himself. *Has the old bastard been right all along?*

But it no longer mattered to him what The Two thought, or whether he was right or wrong. He would not be governed anymore by his grandfather's opinions, one way or the other. He would neither rebel nor obey. He would do the right thing as he himself saw it.

So, lying in darkness beside his pregnant wife on the eve of his thirtieth birthday, Harlan de Vouvray Ward IV became a man at last.

12

The party started again late the following morning and lasted throughout the day. People came and went, they swam and lazed and drank more champagne and ate massive amounts of food and complimented Hal on his new life-style.

"If Marie could cook like this, I'd marry her tomorrow," someone said as Carlee put down another tray on a table by the pool. There was an outraged squeal.

"And who says Marie would marry you?"

"Good point," returned the man in a lazy voice. Carlee recognized him now as Aaron, one of the pit mechanics. "So tell me, Carlee, how'd a bum like my friend Hal get a girl like you? We all thought Sharon would get him in the end, so we're grateful to you. But I'd like to know how he managed it."

Carlee grinned. "He had to marry me. He got me in the family way."

They all laughed. Hal, sprawled on a lounger beside her, lifted a hand and caught her wrist, drawing it to his mouth. "My lucky day," he said softly. Gasping, Carlee glanced down, to find him looking straight into her eyes, his gaze full of messages. Her heart began to beat hard, and she bit her lip and looked away.

He was different in everything he did, from the moment she had woken up this morning to find him standing beside the bed, dressed and smiling down at her.

"Happy birthday," she'd said. He sank down on the edge of the bed and bent and kissed her with a firmness and determination that she couldn't resist. Then she remembered their guests. "Is everybody getting up? I guess they'll want breakfast before they go."

"Most of them won't be up for a while yet, and they won't be leaving, if I know this bunch. It's going to be a long day," said Hal. "There will be a lot of food and drink consumed. You've got two choices—either I can start ordering in now, and we'll just keep it up all day, or we can get some staff in to cook on the premises. Which would you rather?"

"Oh, Hal, I don't mind cooking," she began.

"One choice you do not have is doing all the cooking yourself," he overrode her ruthlessly. "You can supervise if you like, but if the cooking is going to be done here we are getting staff in."

There was a note of command in his voice which she hadn't heard before. "All right," Carlee said meekly.

"I'll ask Robert the under-cook and one of the maids to come down from the big house unless you'd rather have someone from an agency."

"Ask Robert first," she'd agreed.

The tray she set down now, at almost six o'clock, was Italian *bruschetta*—little slices of *ciabatta* bread dipped in olive oil and crushed garlic, baked in the oven and then covered with a variety of scrumptious toppings: pesto and parmesan; garlic mushrooms and grated cheddar; sun-dried tomatoes and feta; cooked red peppers and parsley; salami and olives; chopped fresh tomatoes and capers. People smacked their lips and gobbled them up, muttering compliments.

Champagne was flowing, the kitchen and dining room tables had been brought out to the pool, and two maids from the big house were setting them with the new china and silverware and crystal Carlee and Hal had bought. Hal had lighted candles in little globes all around the pool, and there were more candles to be lit on the tables. Everything had a festive air.

There were twenty-four people, the largest group by far that Carlee had ever cooked for, but Carlee and Robert had discovered a rapport, and the meal was perfect. They followed the *bruschetta* with cold carrot soup, then a luscious lasagna with a massive green salad, and then a giant birthday cake with candles, which was brought in and set down in front of Hal as they all sang Happy Birthday.

He was surprised, Carlee could see. He turned to her with a deep smile in his eyes, then slipped an arm around her and kissed her on the lips, to cheers from the assembled.

The kiss came to an end at last, but not before Carlee's heart had climbed to her lips and communicated its presence to Hal. Her lack of control frightened Carlee, but she was sure—she was almost sure—that Hal's heart had been on his lips, too.

"Make a wish!" someone cried, and when Hal

grinned and nodded, Carlee made a wish, too. As if sensing that, he turned to her.

"Help me blow them out," he said. So they each took a deep breath and, to appreciative applause, blew all the candles out in one long, joint breath.

"Speech!" shouted someone. "Speech!" It was only a joke, but Hal got to his feet, something so unusual that an expectant silence fell on them all.

"Well, I am going to make a speech," he said. "I've got something to tell you all, and since most of the team is here, this seems as good a time as any.

"I'm thirty years old, and as you all know by now, I'm married and soon to become a father. And I'd like to ask you all to drink a toast—" Hal turned and smiled seductively down at Carlee in the candlelight "—to my *wife*."

There was no mistaking the note of pride and possessiveness in his voice, and she caught her breath and bit her lip on a tremulous smile.

"Carlee," he said, raising his glass.

"Awwright!" "Carlee!" "Yeah!" "Great food, Carlee!" "Glad to know you!" the guests chorused around the tables, and drank.

"The Chelven Light team's been together five years now," Hal continued, "and we've had lots of good times, and some great times, and I enjoyed them all. Well," he checked himself with a conscious grin, "most of them."

As he recounted the history of their mutual adventures, triumphs and failures, the team members laughed and cheered, and some groaned, because it was obvious where this was heading now, and it meant the end of an era.

"Times change, and people change, thank God, and everything has its own natural end. And most of you can probably see that this is the natural end for me. I'm hanging up my helmet as of today—" now the groans were loud and sad "—but you all know damned well that you've got a new champion already and don't need me anymore. Congratulations again, John!"

They drank to John Hoight with applause and cheers.

"What are you going to do, Hal?" a couple of voices called.

"Partly just what I've been doing—research and development at the lab. Some of you know I've been working with Bill and Trev here on a project that's very close to my heart, a new engine. We're just about at a point where we can announce success, and there'll be a lot of changes…"

When he finished speaking and sat down, Carlee couldn't look at him, fearing that she might be reading too much into what he had just said and done. The one solution that had never occurred to her was that Hal could give up the dream of the championship and yet go on with the research. Was this because of their conversation last night? Did it mean he'd made up his mind what he wanted, and it turned out to be her and the baby? She was afraid to look into his eyes for the answer.

Someone got to his feet and shouted Hal's name, and he was toasted, and then they cut the cake and poured more champagne, and the evening went on, and still she couldn't look at him.

* * *

The party took on the aspects of a wake. People stood around seriously drinking now, talking about the old days, the wins, the losses, almost as they would have if Hal had died. Hal felt like a man at his own funeral, and when he reflected how easily it might have been just that, he repeatedly had to shake himself out of a sense of unreality.

By midnight it was clear that a dozen people expected to stay the night again, but Hal knew Carlee had about reached her limit for impromptu weekend parties. He ruthlessly got rid of them all, by the simple expedient of summoning a flotilla of courtesy cars from the nearest hotel and pouring his friends into them. Most were too drunk to protest. When the last guest had gone, Hal and Carlee stood in the flickering candle flames and surveyed the wreckage. The tables and chairs had been removed, the dishes had all been done. A few shadows on the water indicated that objects or food would have to be retrieved from the pool in the morning, but for the most part his friends had been remarkably restrained.

"Alone at last," joked Carlee, sinking onto a lounger and relaxing in the night air as Hal went from candle to candle and blew out the myriad little flames.

When there was only starlight glinting on the pool, he came and sat by her side.

"Listen, I want to tell you something," he said simply.

Carlee nodded and waited in silence while the night cast its soft mood over them.

"My last race," Hal began slowly. "Vassily blew a tire and went spinning by right across my path."

"I know," Carlee said fervently, though she had not told him before that she had watched the race.

"You've got two choices in a case like that, Carlee, and what you choose depends on the moment. There's no rule that serves every situation. You go toward the accident, on the assumption that the accident will have moved by the time you get there, or you head away from it."

She remembered the taste of bile as she watched and could only nod helplessly in the darkness, remembering how she had prayed in that moment.

"The thing is, Carlee, normally you make a choice like that *inside* the race, if you know what I mean. It's not unconscious, it's just—a state of mind that's part of the race. Racing is an altered state of consciousness, anyway."

"I understand," she said.

"I guess I tightened my grip on the wheel when I saw what was happening to Vassily, I don't know, all I know is that suddenly everything hurt like hell, my arm, my ribs—and then my concentration was gone, and I was thinking of you. I thought, *Carlee!*

"And just like that, I wasn't in the race, I was outside it. Above it. I could see the whole thing like a symphony, Carlee, I could see everyone's movement around me, and my own, and I knew exactly what choice to make."

Her eyes burned with tears. She didn't trust herself to speak, so she nodded.

"Vassily hit the wall and bounced back out of my way. If I'd made the other choice, if I'd swerved right, I'd have gone straight into him." He heard the gulp of tears in her throat and paused. "All right?"

She sniffed and nodded. "I'm all right."

"The thing is, Carlee, I had a microsecond, and I could have gone either way. And if I'd gone the other way, this would have been my wake tonight, and Vassily's, too. A memorial service on Hal Ward's birthday, you know? And here's what gets me—it would have been the same people, saying the same things."

She sat in startled silence for a moment, absorbing it. "Yes, I see..." she said at last, and she did.

"Until tonight, I just took things for granted, like all the other times I nearly killed myself. You win some, you lose some, and so far I'm still winning. But tonight I realize how close I came, and suddenly I'm damn glad I survived. The way I look at it, Carlee, you saved my life. That means my life belongs to you, isn't that what they say?"

"Hal..."

He turned and made her face him, stroking the tears from her cheek. "I want you to think things over. I've got some things to clear up before we talk again. But—think about things, Carlee. Will you?"

"Yes, Hal," she said.

"I think I've got more to offer you than you know."

"Yes," she said again.

And then, because he knew now what he wanted, he drew her firmly into his arms and kissed her, long and slow and with determined intent. Carlee felt the kiss, and the intent, as a potent drug in every cell, in every sense.

This time it was impossible to say no.

The phone started ringing at six a.m. Someone had phoned a journalist after Hal's speech, and Hal

Ward's unexpected retirement, following on John Hoight's win, was going to be big news.

It was a slow news day. By mid-morning the main road was full of television crews, sports columnists, print journalists and photographers. The property was lined with security guards summoned by The Two.

Fans and excitement seekers slowly swelled their ranks, and by noon, a couple of journalists crept through the security cordon and began combing the estate, looking for Hal, for Carlee—for anyone to photograph or demand a comment from.

It was Carlee they found. She had watched an announcement of the news early in the morning and then had turned the television off, and so she had no idea what was going on. Three people burst through the hedge surrounding the pool just as she came out of it. She was standing rubbing her hair with a towel, and the click of a camera was the first hint she had of their presence.

"Mrs. Ward! Mrs. Ward! Carlee!" they began screaming, and converged on her where she stood by a lounger in her black one-piece, her wet hair loose down her back. Carlee gazed at them for one astonished moment, then reached for her terry robe and slipped it on. She tied the belt tightly and picked up the pool telephone in one smooth gesture.

"We have intruders by the pool," she said curtly when security answered, and it occurred to her that she had grown more used to wealth than she'd realized.

"We're doing our best," said the guard. "They're probably journalists, and not likely dangerous. But there are thrill seekers in the crowd, too, and they may be unpredictable. Get inside the house if you can, Mrs. Ward. I'll try and get a couple of men over there pronto.''

Carlee punched the number of the lab. "Trevor," she said. "Hal there?"

"Problems?" said Hal immediately.

"There are reporters all over the place, Hal. Should I talk to them?"

"Where the hell's security?" he asked.

"Overwhelmed, I think."

"Damn. I should have foreseen this. Hold them off. Give them coffee or drinks and tell them I'll be along. I'll see you in five minutes."

He came striding through the hedge four minutes later, so Carlee knew he must have borrowed Trevor's car. The lab was a fifteen-minute walk away on the other side of the property, and Hal never drove there.

He found her calmly holding court in the kitchen, talking about nothing in particular as she set out coffee cups. Two security men were standing by the doors to the rest of the house, and another half dozen journalists had arrived.

"As you know, Hal turned thirty yesterday, and he made the announcement at his birthday party. Many of the guests were his closest friends," she was saying when he entered.

Hal bit his lip. He had listened to a couple of the news reports this morning, and he recognized, if the reporters did not, that Carlee was quoting them almost verbatim.

"Hi," he said, by way of announcing his presence, and the reporters turned as one man, leaped to their feet and converged on him. Hal kept walking till he got to Carlee's side, kissed her gently on the cheek and slipped an arm around her.

"You guys harassing my wife?" he asked cheerfully.

"Hey, hey, no way!" they chorused guiltily.

Immediately they began to pelter him with questions, and Carlee used the moment to slip away and get dressed. When she got back, everybody, including the security guards, had left. A little amazed at the speed with which Hal had got rid of them, she stepped outside, and the mystery was solved.

He had not got rid of them. They were all out beyond the hedge in the parking area, crowded around a weird-looking car. Cameras were whirring and clicking, and Hal was saying something that had them all spellbound.

Curious, she crossed to his side and stared at the thing they were photographing. Well, if someone intended to win the Grand Prix championship with this, she knew nothing about racing!

"This is our first fully working model," Hal was saying.

"How long have you been working on this?" someone demanded when Hal paused.

"I got interested in fuel cell technology in university," he said. "I set up my own research team before I graduated."

"Hell, that's seven years!" a journalist exclaimed in amazement. "You've been doing this all through the time you were on the Chelven Light team?"

"That's right."

"And this latest breakthrough is the reason for your retirement?"

Hal smiled down at Carlee. "One of them," he said.

13

"Go right in, Hal," said Jenny nervously. "He's been asking for you."

Hal casually saluted The Two's private secretary and strode through the door to his office.

"What the hell is this?" Harlan shouted furiously, waving a piece of paper. His face was red, his eyebrows jumping together like hairy caterpillars in head-to-head combat.

Hal closed the door behind him. "Good morning, TT," he said cheerfully. "I see you got my lawyer's letter."

"Your lawyers! Since when have Allan Lee Ross been your lawyers?" the old man shouted.

"Since George had a problem with conflict of—"

"And what the hell does it mean?" TT hadn't lowered his voice. He held up the letter again and shook it.

"Why didn't you ask George to explain it if you didn't understand?" Hal leisurely crossed the office and sank into a chair. "It means what it says—you have thirty days in which to transfer my father's assets to me. If not, I will begin legal proceedings to challenge you."

At this calm restatement of the offense, The Two lost the leading edge of his fury. He dropped his arm, the caterpillars retired to their corners, the black eyes looked piercingly at his grandson. "You can't do this, boy! It's unwinnable! You'll gobble up your fortune in legal fees. A case like this could go on for years."

"So you told my mother, thirty years ago. Don't expect it to work on me." He returned his grandfather's gaze with a look of level determination that the old man had never seen in his eyes. "I'm not putting up with it any longer, TT. And don't think you'll be using my father's money to pay your own legal fees, because we intend to get an injunction to prevent your doing that."

The Two stared. "It'll get in all the papers. Think of the shareholders! We've never had a scandal!"

Hal laughed. "Well, not for the past eighty years, anyway!"

"You'll ruin Ward Petrochemical!"

"If necessary," said Hal grimly.

Suddenly, tangibly, there was a power shift in the room, though neither of the two participants consciously observed it. Harlan de Vouvray Ward II slumped.

"I've spent my life building this place!" he said pathetically. "You can't do this, b—" But the word *boy* would not come to his lips. "Hal!" he pleaded.

"Allan Lee Ross have drawn up a document that assigns my father's assets to me," Hal said. "Did you get a copy with the letter?"

Harlan de Vouvray Ward II stared for a long, silent moment into his grandson's eyes and read there nothing but firmness of purpose. "You mean it," he said, his hand already unconsciously groping for his pen. "How can you do this to me?"

Hal grinned appreciatively. "It's the Ward blood, Grandfather." He watched while the old man signed away his control of his grandson's life. "Now," said Hal, picking up the document and folding it away in his jacket, "We have a few other things to discuss."

He hadn't shut the old man up so effectively since that day, fourteen years ago, when he had turned up on the doorstep with his ultimatum about high school. Hal wondered where he had lost the thread in between. But it didn't matter anymore.

"You're a twentieth century man, Grandfather, of course you can't see it. Believe me, the combustion engine is a thing of the past. It won't see us into the future," Hal said.

The Two was gobbling with incoherence. "Dammit—the—we built our fortune on the combustion engine. Ward Oil, then Ward Fuels, now Ward Petrochemical! It tells the whole story! And a damn good fortune it's been!"

"You're right," Hal said. "We have to change the name again."

"And you mean to tell me it's this you've been working on all the time we thought you were trying to come up with a superengine to win the Grand Prix championship?"

"It made a good cover story."

"Dammit, you could have told me! Things would have been different if I'd known this!"

Hal only grinned.

"Fuel cells," muttered the old man.

"It works," said Hal. "We know for sure it works. What we need now is investment on a massive scale. But Ward Petrochemical can afford it. We'll come under the Ward umbrella now, that'll simplify things. Ward has been making a profit out of polluting the earth and depleting its resources for long enough. It's time we made an honest contribution to the world's well-being."

"Do you have any idea how much it would cost to install liquid hydrogen pumps in every Ward fuel station in the country? The shareholders will never stand for it," TT tried feebly.

"The shareholders will do whatever you tell them, and always have," said Hal ruthlessly. "And if they don't—what have we kept controlling interest for, all these years, if not for a moment like this?"

As usual, the kitchen was full of the delicious smells of cooking. Carlee looked up and her breath came in with a little gasp. "Hal! Something's happened! What is it?"

His smile flickered around his mouth, but his eyes remained grave. "A lot of changes. I want to talk to you."

"Just let me set this back in the oven," she said, and a minute later she slipped her apron over her head and followed him into the sitting room. He waited for her to sit on the sofa and then settled beside her and turned toward her. After a moment he took her hand in his.

"Carlee, the other night, you said I had nothing to offer you—"

He heard the little intake of breath, saw her teeth catch her lower lip. "I'm sorry," she said softly.

"But you were right. I thought money was all a woman could want, and I've never offered a woman more than that. But I want to offer you more, Carlee."

She smiled as the tears sprang to her eyes. "Do you?"

"I think I've got something to offer you now, Carlee. Will you listen?"

"They're saying that what you've been working on all this time is an electric car, not a racing engine at all," she offered.

"We needed a cover story so we could work without interference." And so at last he began to tell her about the work that had been consuming him for so long. "The big thing is the fuel cell technology."

She listened with wide, fascinated eyes, and he knew what the quality was that Gerry Maitland had seen in her: she heard everything he said without prejudice. She didn't judge by anything she already knew, didn't reject what she couldn't understand. Carlee had that rarest of commodities, a completely open mind.

"So instead of plugging batteries into a charger every night," she recapped, "you carry liquid hydrogen in your tank and that goes through the fuel cell and produces electricity to power the car?"

"And the only by-product is water vapor."

"Hal, it's just wonderful! It's been the top story on all the news broadcasts all day. Everybody's just so excited. The phone's been ringing off the hook with the science journalists—they're annoyed they weren't in on the first announcement, but I agreed you'd have another press conference just for them. It's booked for tomorrow. Oh! and somebody at Ford called! They want talks with you. And Honda, oh—and a German company! I've written down a million messages.''

"I'll look at them later," he said, restraining her as she was about to get up.

Carlee willingly subsided and smiled at him. "What's going to happen next?"

"Ward is going to take the design to a consortium of car manufacturers and invite them to start producing. A significant factor is that we already have the stations in place over half the country—with our affiliated stations, Forbes, we have the mainland covered. All we have to do is install hydrogen pumps at every Ward and Forbes gas station and we've got a workable proposition.''

"Oh, Forbes! A man named Standish called from there.''

"Good.''

"And your grandfather has agreed to all of this?''

"My grandfather as of today is chairman of the board. I'm now president and chief executive officer of the new Ward Energy Systems. All subject to shareholder approval, of course.''

She stared at him. "Wow!" she breathed. "It's all kind of sudden, isn't it?"

"Some of it's sudden," he agreed. "I moved faster than I planned. But I had to show you I could offer you more than just financial security, Carlee.''

She found she couldn't breathe. "Did you, Hal?" she whispered. "Why?"

He put one arm around her and lifted the other to stroke her cheek. "Because I love you. Carlee, I want you to be my wife. I want to be the father of our child. Will you try and make this a real marriage with me?''

She turned on him eyes full of all the love she had never allowed herself to feel, all the love he wanted to see in her.

''Oh, Hal!'' was all she whispered, but that was enough. He swept her into his arms and bent his head to take his wife's mouth in a kiss.

The heat of physical desire flared up between them, and his hands grew more demanding on her body. As she sank back against the sofa in his arms, Carlee warned mischievously, ''The casserole will burn.''

''Carlee,'' said Hal, ''no offense to your cooking, but I have more important things on my mind right now than food.''

Epilogue

"Hal?"

It wasn't much more than a whisper, but he was wide awake in a split second. "Carlee?" He sat up and flicked on the lamp, then turned. She lay on her side, turned away from him. She was sweating and gritting her teeth. He began automatically to rub her back, and for a few moments coached her breathing.

"Oh, thank you!" she breathed in relief as the pain subsided.

"Time to call Phoebe?"

"No, not yet. Soon, probably."

Hal looked at his watch. He was more nervous than any race had ever made him. "Four o'clock. The hell with it, I'm calling her."

"Hal, I really don't need her yet."

"Yeah, but I want her awake when you do," he said, reaching for the phone. Phoebe's number was programmed in. She answered on the second ring.

"Hal Ward," he said. "Carlee's starting her pains."

She arrived two hours later. Carlee was sitting in a body-temperature Jacuzzi with only the lightest of water movement, Hal standing behind, gently massaging her neck.

"Right," said Phoebe, stripping down to a swimsuit without embarrassment. "Let's check your dilation."

Two hours later Hal tenderly dried his wife down and helped her into the bedroom for the birth.

"Push, Carlee, push! Your baby is coming!"

"Oh, God, oh, baby! Hal? Hal?"

"I'm here, Carlee, my love."

"Hal, I can't do it! It hurts so much!"

"Yes, you can, Carlee. For the baby, you can do it. Come on, now, push!"

"Oh, God! Hold my hand!"

"Ohhhh, Hal, isn't she beautiful? Isn't she the most beautiful thing you ever saw?"

"Yes, she is."

"You're crying. Why are you crying?"

"Because she's the most beautiful thing I ever saw, Carlee. Next to you."

"Are you disappointed?" Carlee asked sleepily, several hours later.

"No," said Hal softly. He sat beside the bed, smiling at his just-fed daughter, who, with a sigh of complete trust, was drowsing off to sleep again in his arms. "I didn't realize it before she came, but all the time I was hoping for a girl."

"Your grandfather will be disappointed," Carlee said.

"Probably. It doesn't matter."

"Have you told him?"

"Not yet."

Carlee giggled. "All his manipulations and machinations, all for nothing! No heir to the dynasty after all! I bet you'll enjoy telling him!"

"It adds spice to the general satisfaction," Hal grinned.

"A girl?" The chairman of the board's eyebrows twitched together over his forehead. "She's had a *girl*? How is it we didn't know this before?"

"Because Carlee doesn't like the invasive techniques that tell you the sex of the baby in advance," Hal said calmly.

"I've been assuming all this time that it was a boy!" The Two said indignantly. "We've got the schools lined up, the—"

"Well, you don't need me to tell you about assumptions, TT."

The chairman of the board ignored that, his eyebrows working busily as he stared into the middle distance. Suddenly he slapped his hand on the table.

"By God, why didn't I think of that!" he exploded triumphantly. He focused on his grandson. "I tell you what, Hal, it's the best damn thing that could have happened! A woman! Of course! With all this new eco-friendly technology we'll be taking onboard, it makes sense to have a woman being groomed for the future! The right school, that's the thing! I'll get George onto it! She'll graduate from college in 2020…you can take her right in at management level, probably in environment protection research. Sort of thing women like. And we'll have that department well up and running by then.

"Yes sir, you tell Carlee from me she's done exactly the right thing! After all, Hal, as your French great-great-grandfather used to say—'If you want something said, give it to a man. If you want something done, give it to a woman'!"

* * * * *

Daniel MacGregor is at it again...

New York Times bestselling author

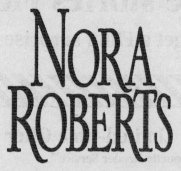

NORA ROBERTS

introduces us to a new generation of MacGregors
as the lovable patriarch of the illustrious MacGregor
clan plays matchmaker again, this time to his three
gorgeous granddaughters in

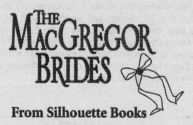

THE MACGREGOR BRIDES

From Silhouette Books

Don't miss this brand-new continuation of Nora Roberts's
enormously popular *MacGregor* miniseries.

Available November 1997 at your favorite retail outlet.

Take 4 bestselling love stories FREE
Plus get a FREE surprise gift!

Special Limited-time Offer

Mail to Silhouette Reader Service™

3010 Walden Avenue
P.O. Box 1867
Buffalo, N.Y. 14269-1867

YES! Please send me 4 free Silhouette Yours Truly™ novels and my free surprise gift. Then send me 4 brand-new novels every other month, which I will receive months before they appear in bookstores. Bill me at the low price of $2.69 each plus 25¢ delivery and applicable sales tax, if any.* That's the complete price and a savings of over 10% off the cover prices—quite a bargain! I understand that accepting the books and gift places me under no obligation ever to buy any books. I can always return a shipment and cancel at any time. Even if I never buy another book from Silhouette, the 4 free books and the surprise gift are mine to keep forever.

201 BPA AZH2

Name	(PLEASE PRINT)	
Address	Apt. No.	
City	State	Zip

This offer is limited to one order per household and not valid to present Silhouette Yours Truly™ subscribers. *Terms and prices are subject to change without notice. Sales tax applicable in N.Y.

USYRT-296   ©1996 Harlequin Enterprises Limited

ELIZABETH AUGUST

Continues the twelve-book series—36 HOURS—in November 1997 with Book Five

CINDERELLA STORY

Life was hardly a fairy tale for Nina Lindstrom. Out of work and with an ailing child, the struggling single mom was running low on hope. Then Alex Bennett solved her problems with one convenient proposal: marriage. And though he had made no promises beyond financial security, Nina couldn't help but feel that with a little love, happily-ever-afters really could come true!

For Alex and Nina and *all* the residents of Grand Springs, Colorado, the storm-induced blackout was just the beginning of 36 Hours that changed *everything!* You won't want to miss a single book.

As seen on TV!

Free Gift Offer

With a Free Gift proof-of-purchase from any Silhouette® book,
you can receive a beautiful cubic zirconia pendant.

This gorgeous marquise-shaped stone is a genuine cubic
zirconia—accented by an 18" gold tone necklace.

(Approximate retail value $19.95)

Send for yours today...

compliments of ▼ *Silhouette*®
™

To receive your free gift, a cubic zirconia pendant, send us one original proof-of-purchase, photocopies not accepted, from the back of any Silhouette Romance™, Silhouette Desire®, Silhouette Special Edition®, Silhouette Intimate Moments® or Silhouette Yours Truly™ title available at your favorite retail outlet, together with the Free Gift Certificate, plus a check or money order for $1.65 U.S./$2.15 CAN. (do not send cash) to cover postage and handling, payable to Silhouette Free Gift Offer. We will send you the specified gift. Allow 6 to 8 weeks for delivery. Offer good until December 31, 1997, or while quantities last. Offer valid in the U.S. and Canada only.

Free Gift Certificate

Name: _____

Address: _____

City: _____ State/Province: _____ Zip/Postal Code: _____

Mail this certificate, one proof-of-purchase and a check or money order for postage and handling to: SILHOUETTE FREE GIFT OFFER 1997. In the U.S.: 3010 Walden Avenue, P.O. Box 9077, Buffalo NY 14269-9077. In Canada: P.O. Box 613, Fort Erie, Ontario L2Z 5X3.

FREE GIFT OFFER   084-KFD

ONE PROOF-OF-PURCHASE

To collect your fabulous FREE GIFT, a cubic zirconia pendant, you must include this original proof-of-purchase for each gift with the properly completed Free Gift Certificate.

084-KFDR

SILHOUETTE WOMEN KNOW ROMANCE WHEN THEY SEE IT.

And they'll see it on **ROMANCE CLASSICS**, the new 24-hour TV channel devoted to romantic movies and original programs like the special **Romantically Speaking—Harlequin™ Goes Prime Time**.

Romantically Speaking—Harlequin™ Goes Prime Time introduces you to many of your favorite romance authors in a program developed exclusively for Harlequin® and Silhouette® readers.

Watch for **Romantically Speaking—Harlequin™ Goes Prime Time** beginning in the summer of 1997.

If you're not receiving ROMANCE CLASSICS, call your local cable operator or satellite provider and ask for it today!

Escape to the network of your dreams.

See Ingrid Bergman and Gregory Peck in *Spellbound* on Romance Classics.

Share in the joy of yuletide romance with brand-new stories by two of the genre's most beloved writers

DIANA PALMER
and
JOAN JOHNSTON
in

LONE STAR
CHRISTMAS

Diana Palmer and Joan Johnston share their favorite Christmas anecdotes and personal stories in this *special hardbound edition.*

Diana Palmer delivers an irresistible spin-off of her **LONG, TALL TEXANS** series and Joan Johnston crafts an unforgettable new chapter to **HAWK'S WAY** in this wonderful keepsake edition celebrating the holiday season. So perfect for gift giving, you'll want one for yourself…and one to give to a special friend!

Available in November at your favorite retail outlet!

Only from

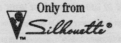